THE SECRET PATHWAY
to
HEALING

The journey of healing relationships
and learning to love yourself

Love and Light
Linda Drake

By Linda Drake
and Abraham

First Edition
First Printing, 2010
Cover art 2010 by Patrick Drake

ISBN: 1452899398
ISBN-13: 9781452899398

ABOUT THE AUTHOR

Linda Drake (Austin, Texas) is an author, teacher and life path healer who has dedicated her life to working with Spirit. She travels worldwide helping people heal the physical and emotional challenges in their lives, including relationship and childhood issues. Linda does her healing work through her books, seminars, workshops, and private sessions. Her guidance focuses on empowerment, knowledge and healing, enabling each of you to create a joyful journey of purpose. Linda acknowledges that it is only through God that she is able to embrace the gifts and purpose she has been given. You can contact Linda through her website, www.LindaDrakeConsulting.com. Visit Linda's website for the latest news and locations of her special appearances.

DEDICATION

I dedicate this book to those that truly wrote it: To the Abraham group, who channeled their amazing knowledge and guidance through me. This is a group of highly evolved spiritual beings, that work as God's messengers to bring humanity the wisdom of God and they call themselves "Abraham". They provide us with a greater understanding of how powerful we are as souls in the human experience. They enlighten us as to how we can create the life that we desire and fulfill the purpose we have chosen for each lifetime. Abraham enables us see our greatest gifts and our most challenging issues. They provide us with the knowledge and tools to overcome life's most challenging hardships and suffering. I am honored that they chose me as the vessel of their knowledge and to be their voice in reaching humanity. I have gratitude that they continue to work through me.

I dedicate this book to the individuals that have shared their stories though our book. They allowed Abraham and myself to touch their lives in a unique way. These individuals worked with the tools that Abraham gave them, to change their lives, to heal the darkness and empower the light within them. We have gratitude to them for graciously sharing with us a glimpse of their real life challenges and their journey of healing. Their stories have given us a message of hope. They have blessed you with the knowledge they have gained, as they too are messengers for God's work.

It is only through love that we are able to heal ourselves and God's love is the source of all creation. It is through God's guidance that we are able to fulfill our life purpose and create the life that we desire.

Last, but certainly not least, I dedicate this book to my husband, Pat Drake. He truly is an angel in my life. He supports me in all of the work that God has given me to do. Throughout the long hours of work and the long trips as we reach out to those across the country, he has been by my side. He supports me physically, emotionally and mentally, as life can be quite crazy for me at times. He continually shows me how to laugh at life and myself. He has the patience of an angel, so I am quite sure that God specifically designed him just for me.

At some point in your life, I hope all of you are blessed with a life partner as wonderful as mine. He always finds the best in me, even when I can't find it. His confidence in me enhances my strength. God truly blessed me in this lifetime and I am grateful.

Love and Light
Linda

TABLE OF CONTENTS

INTRODUCTION ix

CHAPTER 1 1
LINDA'S EXPERIENCE WITH SPIRIT

CHAPTER 2 - THE LIFE PLAN 21
THE CHOICES AND CHALLENGES OF YOUR ISSUES

CHAPTER 3 39
THE CHILD WITHIN YOU

CHAPTER 4 51
THE ROLE OF BELIEF SYSTEMS

CHAPTER 5 63
TRUST & ABANDONMENT

CHAPTER 6 85
ABUSE, CONTROL & JUDGMENT

CHAPTER 7 111
LOVE, RESPONSIBILITY, ADDICTIONS

CHAPTER 8 141
PAST LIVES & CURRENT ISSUES

CHAPTER 9 169
RESTORING THE JOY OF THE INNER-CHILD

CHAPTER 10 185
SOUL GROUPS AND SOUL MATES

CHAPTER 11 205
HEALING YOURSELF - THE TOOLS AND THE PROCESS
REIKI & CHAKRAS

CHAPTER 12 227
RELATIONSHIPS - WHY THEY ARE SO IMPORTANT

"THE JOURNEY OF FORGIVENESS ENABLES
YOU TO WALK THE PATHWAY TO LOVE"
Linda Drake

INTRODUCTION

This Introduction and the first chapter tell about my life and my experiences with Spirit. From the second chapter on, it is all about you. The knowledge that Abraham (who is the spiritual group that I work with) shares in our book is to help you gain a better understanding of your life: your past, your present, and the opportunity to create the life of your dreams.

Some of the life experiences we share may be as challenging for you to believe as they were for me, but they are all true. I am not trying to force you to believe anything that challenges your belief system – but what if...?

Accept what you are comfortable with and file the rest away to reconsider when you are ready. This is the same advice that Abraham gave me because I was such a skeptic at the beginning of my adventure with Spirit. All this "woo-woo stuff" scared me because I did not understand the spirituality in it. However, after too many experiences and confirmations to ignore, I now admit that this "woo-woo stuff" makes perfect sense to me. It has answered many of the questions that I have been challenged with all of my life.

The spiritual connection I now have in my life has brought an understanding to things that I had questioned all of my life. The joy and comfort I have received by knowing that God walks hand in hand with us through our chosen journey in life has given me the confidence to do my work. I have experienced God's unconditional love, and I want you to share in this joy.

To avoid any confusion as you read, let me pause now to explain the difference between capitalized "Spirit" and lower case "spirit." When I am referring to the God consciousness I will use "Spirit" with a capital "S." But when I am referring to the soul of humans, which are in spirit form, I will also use the word "spirit," with a small "s."

My life at this time is not "normal" by any means. From the time Spirit made their presence known to me, the experiences of my life have been like "hanging on to the tail of a wild horse," as I never know what to expect next. I once read that "normal" was only a setting on a washing machine. How true that is for my life! At times my life appears quite typical, as I immensely enjoy my roles of wife, mother and grandmother. To meet me on the street, you wouldn't notice anything unusual about me, but the experiences of my life are far from what others would consider normal. Some people call what I do "weird," and to them it may be, but to me, it is just another day in the adventure of life. Who wants to be a washing machine anyway?

I work with Spirit doing healing work. We work together helping people understand and overcome the challenging issues of their lives. We deal with both childhood issues and relationship issues.

As Spirit's instrument of healing, I allow Spirit to work through me. I also work with Abraham in channeling their messages of wisdom. Abraham is the collective consciousness of a group of highly evolved spiritual beings. Their job is to connect humanity with the wisdom of God. This wisdom is provided to us so that we might overcome the challenges that sabotage our lives. For much of our existence, humanity has prayed to God asking for direction and Abraham's group is one of the many spiritual groups meant to bring us God's wisdom.

I absolutely love doing my healing work, so stopping long enough to write this series of books has been a real challenge. Spirit explained to me (the stubborn one, they call me) that it wasn't physically possible for me to reach out and heal the world one person at a time, but I could send Spirit's words of instruction out through this book to enable others to heal their own lives.

For many years now I have been doing healing work with Spirit and have had some amazing experiences. I had absolutely no intention of writing a book, but Spirit kept insisting that I share my own spiritual development and our experiences as well as the healing experiences of my clients with humanity. As I sat down to begin writing these books, I was joined by a group of beings that introduced themselves as Abraham.

I had been working with Abraham for 6 years at this point, so I was very familiar with their messages. But before this time I did not realize that they were a group consciousness. As we worked together, they would talk and I would write, astonished at the knowledge they were sharing. Spirit would join in our writing sessions to add their own words of wisdom and explanations for me.

My fingers would fly over the keys of my computer keyboard as their words would miraculously form sentences, paragraphs, chapters and finally to my amazement, a completed book.

When Spirit began working with me, I asked for an explanation of who "Spirit" was. They introduced themselves as the combination of God energy, the Masters and the Angelic Realm. Throughout this book, I will refer to this fantastic combination as "Spirit."

I am sure you are wondering how I hear the messages given to me by Spirit. I have heard chatter going on in my head all of my life, like some of you. It is like standing in a crowed room and hearing many conversations at once, except that I hear it loudest when I am all alone. When I first realized that I could slow down the chatter and focus on what I was hearing, the messages began to make sense. I was receiving messages from my spirit guides and realized that I had been hearing them all my life.

Many of their messages would come through as thoughts that I recognized and used in my daily life, thinking that it was just my own common sense. That is how most of us unconsciously work with our own spirit guides.

Once I started pursuing my spiritual path, I learned to fine tune my receptors to hear more, just as you would a radio, tuning from static to audible words. I then began to hear Spirit and my spirit guides talk with me just as I hear people in physical form me talk.

I frequently work with the collective consciousness of Abraham, as I do many of the Masters. They are all messengers of God that channel their wisdom and healing through me. Through working with their energy, Spirit has taught me to receive spiritual messages and healing energies and to relay them to others.

Sometimes I hear their words before I share them but usually they speak directly through me. In channeling with Abraham, they work in both ways. I have agreed to allow many different spiritual beings and those of the angelic realm to direct their healing energies through my physical body for the well-being of those they are working with.

The methods of healing that Spirit taught me are powerful, and we desire to share them with the world. In this book I will include true stories that my clients have written about their experiences, to show examples of real life issues. Of course their names will be changed for privacy but the rest of the story will be left as written.

Sometimes it is hard to understand how an issue demonstrates itself in your own life until you hear how someone else has experienced it. Through their stories, clients have generously agreed to share their healing experiences. You will laugh and you will cry as these stories touch your heart.

You may read the same sentence several times throughout this book, but this is not by mistake. The idea being repeated is so important to your healing that Spirit wants to plant the memory of that idea in your soul.

Abraham chose me to channel their messages and they write their books thorough the perspective of human experiences so that their messages can be easily understood by all of us. Many other books have been channeled by highly evolved spiritual beings, yet their assistance is not revealed.

In the case of Abraham's series of healing books, I give full credit to the Abraham group and the guidance of Spirit. Anyone that knows me personally could assure you that it is definitely not based on my knowledge. I've had to learn from Abraham and Spirit just as you do.

CHAPTER 1
LINDA'S EXPERIENCE WITH SPIRIT

At the time when Spirit entered my life, I didn't know what a spiritual path was, much less the life changing adventure that I was embarking on. The spiritual world was a complete mystery to me.

My name was Skeptic, with a big capital "S." Although I was raised with a strong religious background, I always felt there was some aspect of religion or God that I just wasn't understanding, or maybe there was more to it that I wasn't being told. I found myself questioning many things because of knowledge and feelings that I couldn't explain.

As a country girl from a small Texas town outside of Austin, I grew up in a traditional world. Being an animal lover, my greatest treasure was my horse Blazer, with whom I spent hours everyday. Looking back, I can remember many unusual events in my childhood, but I just accepted them and went on believing that those things happened to everyone. I married young, became the mother of two fantastic daughters and built a successful business with my husband, again believing my life to be pretty normal.

Throughout my life I often had experiences of *deja vu* and dreams that came true. I just knew things, but I attributed them to "feminine intuition" as I didn't know any different.

Then, after eighteen years of marriage and motherhood, I found myself divorced and totally confused about where my life was going. With the knowledge that Abraham has now provided me, I look back understanding how I created each experience to learn about my issues. That sounds so much better than thinking "Man, did I screw up my life!" It is also more accurate.

As everyone does, I had to experience many life lessons and challenges. There were numerous bumps on my road of life. I only wish I knew then what I know now.

We all say that, but the knowledge I now have about life issues would have really helped me to understand my life and the people in it. I would have understood why I created my life as it was and I would have been able to identify the beliefs that were forming within me. These beliefs created the pattern of experiences that would continue to unfold throughout my life.

As we all do, I made a lot of choices and decisions that I thought were mistakes. I now recognize those "mistakes" were in reality opportunities to learn about myself and to grow. Without those particular experiences and those particular people around me, I would not be the person I am today. And, I truly love who I am today!

When I was at that lowest emotional time in my life, Spirit brought to me an angel in human form named Pat Drake. I didn't understand the significance of what was happening. I thought that a big part of my life had ended, I didn't know who I was and I couldn't envision a future for me. Spirit and my higher-self had formulated a plan for me that I could never have imagined for myself.

If I had known to trust in Spirit during the early years of my life, things would have been much easier for me. It was at this point that Spirit reintroduced me to Pat Drake, a man from my past. We had been great friends while growing up, riding horses together and sharing long talks.

Now I understand how he was part of my destiny as Spirit brought him back into my life at this particular time to provide me with the unconditional love and unfailing support that I desperately needed. A soul mate had entered my life and I had no idea how important he would become to me. I am still amazed at how our lives work and how Spirit always knows what we need, even when we don't.

It would take a very special person to provide me the support that I would need considering what Spirit had in store for me. Just prior to this man reentering my life, I had become extremely ill, terribly crippled with pain and unexplainable illnesses. After being sent to twelve different doctors, it was through a channeled message of guidance from my aunt that we discovered I had Fibromyalgia and Lupus. I was then directed to the right doctor. I was soon to learn the trauma that both of these diseases can bring. I was unable to work because of the fog of confusion and terrible migraines.

Regular cortisone injections in my back were the only thing that enabled me to walk or to move about. My hands were curled shut, clinched with pain. I suffered with endometriosis, irritable bowel syndrome, diseased thyroid as well as many other mysterious symptoms. Consequently, I was depressed and scared of the direction my life was going.

This combination of symptoms made no sense to the doctors. I was already a medical mess when the Lupus disease decided to kick my butt as it began attacking my body. The bright spot in my life came when that angel whom Spirit had brought back into my life courageously became my husband, patiently supporting me through all of my pain and suffering.

It was a devastating battle that went on for five years.

I did a tremendous amount of praying during this time. The doctors and the long list of medications they prescribed weren't able to help much, so I turned to my faith in God. God and I had some pretty long talks that I felt we both cried through. I had been praying for Him to show me a way to heal my own illness as well as a way to heal others who were suffering in the same way I was.

Be careful what you ask for, because your prayers <u>will</u> be answered. The answers may not come as you expect, but God will give you what he knows you need for your chosen path. Trust in Him, as your words to his ears are always powerful.

My prayers were answered, but in a very unusual way: while in prayer I kept hearing the words, "Take the gift, we'll heal your pain."

I heard this in various ways, but I always focused on the part of "…we'll heal your pain." I didn't understand, but in desperation I screamed out to this whispered voice, "Whatever, just do it! Take away my pain!"

A feeling spread through me that I have never been able to explain, but I instantly knew something significant had happened to me. My guides and angels now tell me that there was a great party and celebration among them when it was finally "the time" for me to walk my spiritual path. I had unknowingly agreed to what would soon become an interesting and amazing future for me. I am sure my spirit/higher-self knew the path they were offering me, but my human consciousness would never have agreed to something, which at the time seemed so weird. Remember, at that time I still thought I was "normal."

After five years of my body experiencing such horrible pain that I just wanted to die, the pain was gone, absolutely gone. I couldn't believe how quickly the medical condition of my body had changed. In a matter of days there was dramatic improvement with more to come as time went on.

I didn't know what to attribute the change to, with my logical mind I began searching for answers but there were none. I even thought that maybe the medicines I had been taking for five years had finally begun to work. I ultimately resolved to accept that it truly was a miracle created by God. I thanked God daily, as I still do, for the miraculous recovery.

There are many aspects of these diseases that the doctors do not understand, but they do know that these diseases don't just disappear. There is no cure for either disease -- only treatments. My doctors were baffled, stating that perhaps both illnesses had gone into a state of remission.

Miraculously that remission has now lasted for more than ten years. The pain and illnesses associated with those diseases were totally gone. THIS WAS A MIRACLE FROM GOD! Yes, God does bring us miracles, but only when we are ready to receive them.

After this miraculous healing occurred, it was obvious to everyone around me that something had happened that I could not explain. I just said that I prayed for healing, and that God answered my prayers. At that time I left out the part about Spirit talking to me. At first I would pray my words of "Thank you for the blessings," quickly closing before the voices started talking again.

It was after several weeks and continued confirmation that I dared still myself long enough to hear the voice again.

When I asked who was speaking to me, they introduced themselves as Spirit. I asked who Spirit was and they defined themselves this way: the consciousness of God the Divine Source, the Angels that are the fingers of God that work within our lives, and the Masters that bring us the messages of God.

Spirit spoke in a very comforting way that released all of my fears, except for the fear that I had lost my mind, and that thought kept creeping into my daily conversations with Spirit. I didn't dare share this experience with others as they would surely think I was crazy!

I suspiciously continued to talk with Spirit as I wasn't sure how this all worked, asking hundreds of questions, but still being in denial that I was to be the healer that they expected me to be. They kept telling me to be patient, as the journey of my life would soon be revealed. This just irritated me because at that time I had very little patience.

When I reached the point that I was able to clearly communicate with my own spiritual guides, one of my first questions was "What the hell was that painful experience all about?" Please pardon my language – it was a very emotional talk! They told me that my higher-self/soul had created the experience for me. Wow, did that suggestion make me mad! I started spouting off before they could get another word out.

"Are you telling me that I chose to be in all that pain? Why would I have ever chosen an illness that created so much physical pain and illness that I was often tempted to take my own life? If I needed to learn something, couldn't I have just caught a really bad cold?"

My guides patiently explained that the illnesses taught me the depths of despair to which pain can carry the physical being.

As you can see from my conversations with Spirit, I desperately tried to sabotage our relationship by pushing them away from me. I was skeptical of everything they told me. I eventually discovered that my skepticism was a front for my fear, as I was afraid of failure. Spirit seemed to see something in me that I could not see or was afraid to see. Instead of embracing the confidence that they had in me, I was looking for a way out of our agreement. I challenged Spirit on everything that they told me. I needed proof in an area that was built on faith. I must admit that Spirit came through on every challenge and every promise they made to me.

My experience had taught me to have compassion for others, and that compassion would become an important tool for me as a healer. Spirit's healing of my physical body taught me to believe in the power of prayer and the miracles that God can bring to us. We are taught to give responsibility for our health to doctors and the pharmaceutical medications that they push at us, thus having no responsibility for our own health and healing. I've been taught that Pharmaceutical medications.

When we close our minds to alternative sources of healing, we miss the opportunity to discover the root of the problem. Because of our limited thought, we miss the real opportunity to heal. My work is now focused on helping others understand and overcome their struggles with the physical, mental and emotional challenges of their life.

Through Spirit's direction we have discovered where and how illnesses are attached to emotional issues. This knowledge has enabled us to help thousands of individuals to understand and heal the journey they are currently on. This knowledge is what we are going to share with you throughout this book.

Soon after I was set free from my pain, Spirit's plan went into action. At that time our lives were by no means calm: we had a rebellious teenage step-daughter and a mother-in-law with a broken leg living with us.

So when I was invited to join Elaine Ireland, a local psychic, on a trip to Denver, I thought it would be both interesting and educational. While in Denver, I went with her to a psychic/metaphysical fair just to play around. I wasn't sure if I really believed all that stuff, but still it was fun.

At the fair I walked around suspiciously, looking at the many people claiming to be "psychic." The first one I felt attracted to was Kat Darden, whom I later found out was one of the best psychics in the country.

The first thing out of her mouth was, "You have healing hands."

My reaction, as a quickly hid my hands, was "What the heck does that mean?"

She told me to pursue my intuitive path because I had been given a healing gift from God. I walked away thinking "Oh sure, me a gift to heal."

Yet I wondered, how had she known about the miraculous healing that Spirit had created for me and the messages I had been given, when I had not told her anything about myself.

I continued to search through the fair for other psychic readers to whom I felt drawn. By the end of the day I had experienced five readings and been told by five different psychics that I was gifted with "healing hands." The first few I was able to laugh about, thinking "No thank you, not my thing." But by the time I got to the fifth one, I'll admit I was getting scared.

I didn't know what this "healing stuff" was about, but I was sure I didn't want anything to do with it. My psychic friends just laughed at my distress, because my friend Elaine had told me, in a psychic reading years before, that I too had psychic gifts. I didn't want to hear about it then and I wasn't ready now.

I left the fair in total confusion, yet hanging on to my thoughts of denial. I just wanted to get back home--rebellious step-daughter, broken legged mother-in-law, and all!

Leaving Denver to return to Austin, we stopped at a restaurant that was many miles from the fair. A complete stranger approached me with a message. He very calmly said, "God sent me to tell you that He has given you the gift of healing and not to be afraid because He will teach you how to use it." This man then calmly turned and walked away.

You can imagine how completely stunned I was. This was getting way too weird for me!

I was sure a mistake had been made; God could not have chosen anyone more down-to- earth and simple than me. Now I was really scared, because I had to return home and explain to my husband, mind you, who had just gone through five years of hell with me and my health issues, what had happened during my four-day vacation.

Upon arriving home, still in my own disbelief, I sat him down to try to explain the events of my weekend and what I had been told. This is a man that is just as analytical and stable as they come, yet he calmly looked at me and said, "Linda, I love you and whatever makes you happy is fine with me."

Note that I had just told this man that I was being recruited by God to do healing work for him! Any one else would have called the mental hospital to have me picked up and carted away, but my beautiful husband was and is my angel.

Of course, he now admits he was thinking, "What next?" But he supported me then, as he still does. This was all very new to me; yet it was somewhat familiar in that it began to explain my previously unexplainable experiences with *deja vu* and prophetic dreams, as well as that feeling of just "knowing things" with no explanation of how I knew them.

For most of my life I had been aware that my hands would get very hot and tingly for no apparent reason. I never thought much about it, just as I never thought much about the many strange things I knew, felt, or did throughout my life, because I considered myself "normal." This was just the beginning of my many adventures, as my life would soon take a sharp turn, veering away from "normal."

God fulfilled his promise: he did teach me.

He surrounded me with the best spiritual teachers possible. There were many intuitive teachers that Spirit placed around me to help me through my fears. This was only the beginning of a grand adventure.

As I began to go to my Angels and Guides for help. I learned I had to "still" myself long enough to listen. I did this through meditation, which was a challenge for me, just as it may be for many of you; I had a very difficult time quieting my mind. Every time I sat down, my mind would be filled with tasks I needed to do, or worse yet, things I had forgotten to do.

My spiritual teachers taught me to use guided meditation to build the connection with my spirit guides and Angels. I continue to use meditation daily for many purposes. Eventually, I learned to just talk with them in a conversational manner. Don't think I wasn't still questioning whether I was losing my mind, as that thought was a regular occurrence--and still is at times when I find myself in unbelievable situations.

I had to overcome my logical mind and learn to accept that I really was hearing Spirit talk to me.

Many other strange things began happening to me, and I mean on a daily basis. At least these things had not been a part of my previously "normal" life. I would sit in a trance for eight hours at a time, while Spirit worked with me, educating my mind and preparing my body to work with the high vibrational energy that I would be channeling. This educational process became a regular routine for me.

My husband would return home each day to my greeting of, "You won't believe what happened today." It was both exciting and scary. I was given the message to take Reiki. I didn't know what Reiki was, but I was soon to learn. I have to say that the Reiki Method of healing has been, and is, one of the most powerful things I have ever done!

The Reiki knowledge and energy truly changed my life, opening my life up to a whole world of gifts that I possessed but did not understand. Reiki is a vibrational healing energy that Spirit channels through me. Anyone can learn to use Reiki as you are empowered to channel the energy through an attunement. Spirit taught me to use my own healing gifts combined with the powerful universal energy of Reiki to assist others on their path to healing. I now include "Spirit healing" to my other methods of healing. (You will read more about the Reiki method of healing in Chapter Nine of this book.)

Being the impatient soul that I am, I continued to ask for my gifts to develop more quickly and more intensely. And I also asked especially to have a greater understanding of the whole picture. I still had many questions, which I asked daily, and I received answers to questions I was yet to think of. You know-- all those questions that you want to ask God when you go home.

Spirit promised to continue working with me, and I agreed to be their vessel, the tool that they could work through, as well as the mouthpiece through which they could channel their messages and knowledge.

I still get scared and wonder, "What was I thinking?" I occasionally go into my worthiness issues, and feel panicked, thinking, "What if they (Spirit) figure out that they have chosen the wrong person? Who am I to think I am special enough to work with Spirit?"

It is at this point that I hear laughter and a voice saying, "You (humans) are all worthy of working with Spirit, as you are all one with God." The first time I heard this, I just sat stunned, processing what I had heard, replaying their words over and over in my mind. Well, I felt much better after that!

To this day, I still have those moments, and Spirit's message is still the same. That message is so reassuring for me and I know that have been blessed in many, many ways.

Spirit provided me with the perfect human spiritual teachers and surrounded me with like-minded friends with whom to share my weird and exciting experiences. Most importantly, my husband loves and supports me as I/we travel around the world doing Spirit's work. I thank God daily for the many blessings he has given me. My husband, family, and friends, as well as my clients-they are all part of my support system along with my Angels and Guides. They all love me and bring so much joy to my life.

A short after my adventure with spirit began, I was told by Dale Clardy, a very gifted medium, that I would be channeling Abraham. Being new to all of this and still thinking that I was in control, my response was that I didn't know who Abraham was and I didn't know what channeling was, but I was pretty sure I didn't want to do it. She just laughed and replied, "You and Abraham will share many new adventures together," and she was right.

It was only a short time after that message that a new voice began talking to me. He introduced himself to me as Abraham the teacher that I had requested. This was the beginning of a great friendship, as we began our work together. We began by building my trust in them and everything that was happening to me.

Abraham was teaching me how to channel their messages to individuals and large groups. I first had to learn to trust them so that I could my get my thoughts and will out of the way and allow them to talk or write through me. It was through hours and hours of joint interaction that I learned to trust Abraham. It was their tremendous love, patience and compassion for humanity that persuaded me.

I was also taught to channel Abraham's guidance for my clients in individual sessions. Their messages held wisdom far beyond anything I consciously knew. I discovered Abraham to be a group consciousness within the spiritual realm that is working with humanity to raise our consciousness. I also discovered that they were great writers, as they channeled a big portion of this series of healing books.

When I first began working with Spirit, I made it very clear that my previous life experiences were pretty traditional and I had little or no knowledge of the spiritual world that they talked about or of their alternative methods of healing.

I still wasn't sure if I believed all that they were telling me, because again, I am talking with a voice that claimed to be coming from God. I had absolutely no experience with connecting with my angels and spirit guides, nor did I understand at that time their importance in my life.

Spirit had given me no time to prepare by taking metaphysical or alternative healing classes or even reading books related to the subject. In fact, I was told not to worry as they would supply me with all of the knowledge I needed. So my education has come from Spirit, as they became my encyclopedia of the spiritual world. I continually bombard them with questions, requesting that they answer me in very simple terms; this is how I will share my knowledge with you.

Spirit told me I would be one of the many Life Path Healers that they were developing in the world. Our purpose is to assist people in discovering and healing the issues that are creating blockages in their lives. These blockages prevent us from having the health, wealth, happiness and fulfillment that we desire in our lives.

Spirit explained that they would give me many different gifts to use in the purpose of healing. Spirit taught me to use my gifts of clairvoyance and clairaudience, as well as learning to use all of my senses to receive messages. Spirit also taught me to open the doorway to the other side and allow those in spirit to communicate with me. I have found this God-given gift to be one of my most valued healing tools, as this communication can bring healing to those in both the physical world and those in the spiritual world.

In one of my previous books, *Reaching Through the Veil to Heal*, this subject is addressed in a more complete and informative way. Grief is often an obstacle for our lives that we have little understanding of. Any type of loss within our lives can and often does create some degree of grief, and without awareness of the symptoms and affects of the grief our lives can quickly be sabotaged and crippled. Whether it is the loss of a job, the ending of a relationship, the death of a beloved pet or loved one to death. Any of these events can changes us and our lives.

Understanding about loss and grief prepares us to experience the unexpected losses as well as the inevitable losses in our lives.

As our work together progressed, Spirit introduced me to the subject of past lives. Now, that was a subject that challenged my belief system!

Nowhere in the limitations of my traditional religious beliefs was I taught about reincarnation. In my beliefs, when you died you went to Heaven and waited for Judgment Day to be reunited with your loved one. So Spirit had to overcome my skepticism about people having past lives.

They referred me to Dr. Brian Weiss' books for the logically proven perspective. I was intrigued by the knowledge that Dr. Weiss shared, but this just caused more questions as I wanted to know more details of the importance of our past lives in relation to what we are currently experiencing.

Being the inquisitive one that I am, I asked Spirit, "Are we required to keep coming back to experience multiple lifetimes? Who is requiring this and why would we want or need to do it?" They explained to me that God desires for us to return home to be embraced in his arms of unconditional love and we return to this state of bliss between each lifetime, but we must also strive for the advancement of our soul. Our souls are striving to evolve to the awareness of God and this is accomplished through the advancement and evolution of the soul.

As souls having the human experience, we must work through our many issues-experiencing them, learning about them and overcoming the negative aspects of these issues. This is how our spirit is meant to evolve.

Negative experiences with our issues frequently create the self-belief that we are not worthy of God's "unconditional love" and that we are flawed, which is far from the truth. We must continue working with these issues while helping others work through theirs, all souls striving to be in a place in which we can love everyone unconditionally.

Judging by humanity's current actions, we have a ways to go, but I trust that with Spirit's help, we will achieve this awareness.

Spirit demonstrated our soul's journey to me as being similar to a pyramid, with each step representing a challenging lesson with one or more of our issues. If we succeed in the challenge, we move up one step. If we fail to understand the lesson and resist learning to overcome the negative aspect of it, we remain on that step waiting for the next opportunity.

We do this work through many lifetimes, each time returning to overcome what we had previously failed to learn about. When we work our way to the top, we will be of the consciousness and spiritual vibration to remain by God's side as long as we desire. We can choose to remain there, or we can choose to return to Earth as spirit guides or Masters to assist others in their life challenges.

Spirit has provided me with many different methods of healing, as we each have different needs and learn in different ways.

I now find that Spirit's guidance and assistance is always available for me. I have learned to trust in this. Often while doing our work together, there may be Ascended Masters, those from the Angelic realm or loved ones in spirit who join us to participate in the healing process.

Clients are often able to feel the invisible, multiple sets of hands touching them while I am working on them. I admit that at this point little would surprise me. I have witnessed the miracles that Spirit can bring to all of us. It has been shown to me that there is a purpose for every experience. I do not have a magic wand to wave over you, but Spirit will use my voice to bring you words of wisdom that will touch your heart in a very powerful way, giving you the opportunity to have awareness of what you could not understand before.

We cannot heal you, but we can give you the knowledge to release the blockages that prevent you from healing yourself. This knowledge and method of healing has been channeled from Spirit for you through this book and the many others in the series of healing books that they are writing.

You may not be ready for the messages of instruction that Spirit has provided in this book. These messages are extremely powerful tools that will challenge you to examine your life and view your relationships in a very different way. But then again, you would not be reading this book if you did not somehow feel that there is a gaping hole of emptiness within your life, or maybe it is a crack that is widening day by day. Either way, you have already begun searching for answers.

Whether your situation is focused on the fact that you are sabotaging your financial future by working in a job below your potential, or you feel trapped in an unhappy relationship that is not meeting your needs, there is hope for fulfillment if you are ready to do the work necessary.

Yes, it will involve change. Change of your negative thought process, your negative beliefs and your negative actions as these are the factors that have created the situation you are currently experiencing.

Most people delay facing their unhappiness because they are afraid of the unknown. This fear is understandable yet it is the biggest challenge you must overcome to achieve all that you desire and to create the energy of change within you. The intent that you set with the universe directs what you will receive within your life. The universe must clearly understand your desires. If you cannot envision prosperity, love and happiness for your life, you embrace the beliefs that you do not deserve them. In this book we will provide you with the tools of empowerment and the instructions for using these tools. These tools will provide assistance in helping you to make the changes necessary to achieve all that you desire for your life.

Look at the situations you are currently experiencing. Is there room for improvement? Are you living up to your full potential? Why would you deny yourself the opportunity of using these tools of empowerment to bring healing for your life?

Some of the methods that we teach are similar to traditional methods; we just use them for your healing process in different ways. We will take you beyond what is sometimes viewed as limitations of the traditional theories of overcoming the challenges of your life, to expand your awareness of the soul's journey and to find appreciation for what you came into this lifetime to experience.

The knowledge we share with you may challenge your belief systems, but obviously you are ready to have them challenged, as the traditional methods many of you have used in the past have not provided you with the type of transformation you desire for your life.

Spirit and Abraham are channeling this book through me. It is primarily written by them but you will find parts that are written by me and my clients to help you connect with the reality of the information. Our goal is to give you the knowledge and tools you need to heal your life. These tools will enable you to release and heal issues of past and present relationships, child-hood relationships, as well as past life issues.

This book is full of real life stories. We are sharing them with you so that you can see the personal side of our healing work. I have changed the names for privacy purposes. Their stories are heartfelt and left unedited so that you can understand the emotions of their experience.

I will be using terms that may not be familiar to you--terms like the inner-child (see Chapter 3), past life regression (see Chapter 8), or communicating with the other side. I have included definitions throughout the chapters to explain these terms in context.

CHAPTER 2
THE LIFE PLAN-
THE CHOICES AND
CHALLENGES OF YOUR ISSUES

In the beginning, the Divine Source, which I will refer to as God, created the heavens and the earth.

Next was His biggest challenge: creating humanity.

Each soul that God creates is an aspect of God, divinely created in all of God's perfection. The harmony and accordance of God's creation goes beyond our meager understanding.

However, I am told by Spirit that God bestowed upon humanity the ability to co-create. Of course, none of us can create as our God created the heavens and the earth. But each of us has the ability to create within our own lives. In other words, we were given free will.

Free will not only involves choosing our own path, but the free will to make choices along the way and to take responsibility for those choices.

Many of you have come to the point in your lives where you are searching for your life's purpose, questioning why you are here. Over time these same questions have been asked by millions of people, so don't think that you are alone in your search-nor are you alone when you feel stuck and frustrated with where you are in your life. This feeling of frustration is created by your spirit/higher-self so that you will begin searching for answers, prompting you to begin making changes to the negative patterns in your life that are no longer working.

The idea, as I am told by Abraham, is for humans, before they are born, to design a blue print for their life, their own life plan.

But there are some guidelines. You are required to have a purpose, and the issues you chose to work on in this lifetime dictate that purpose. Your life plan will hold many options and choices that you will make throughout your life.

These choices could take your life in many different directions; you are in charge and this is how you create the path you will follow. As humans, we like to blame our challenges on God's will, but he didn't create those challenges - we did. The issues you will work with are decided upon before you enter this life.

The direction those issues take is up to you. It's also important to work through and heal any karma you have created while experiencing your previous lifetimes. In your life plan, you have the opportunity to create what you need to experience in this lifetime.

Before we go any further, I will explain *karma*. I am sure you have often heard the saying, "What goes around comes around." This is so true. This statement embodies the meaning of karma. Karma is an energy that you have the choice of creating. Whatever energy that you demonstrate, whether positive or negative, will come back to you in that same way.

This is a universal law, and this energy can come back to you in the same lifetime that it was created or it may be experienced throughout many lifetimes.

Every action, word and thought has an energy connected to it consequently creating karma. For example, when you carry judgment in your heart for a person or race of people, that judgment will always come back to you.

You will be put in a position to suffer a similar judgment or you will be given the opportunity to relive the situation making different choices. If the thought or action is projected with a negative intention, it will come back just as painfully or damaging. This is God's way of allowing us to learn our lessons.

One such lesson is to treat others as you would want to be treated. God will not judge us, but he will allow us to learn through karma. Even a child learns karma. If a child hits another child and that child hits him back harder, he learns about karma very quickly; but if they hug each other and there is forgiveness, they learn how to heal karma.

In our lives, as we send out love and positive energy to others, that same energy will come back to us. In this same manner, putting out negative thoughts and energies to others will bring that negativity back into our lives. I am told by Spirit that anytime we sincerely ask in prayer for blessings for someone, it produces an energy of love that is returned ten-fold.

Do not despair if negativity comes your way. Just know that you are resolving karma that you had previously created. Nothing happens by accident, so perceiving the situation in this positive way allows you to receive the benefit of the karmic resolution and to move forward to create positive energy in you life.

Your life plan will consist of the issues you choose to work with, as well as the people with whom you will interact. Your issues, your karma and the souls with whom you have chosen to interact are the combination that will create the experiences of your lifetime.

As a spark of God, you are empowered to manifest all that you desire for the fulfillment of your destiny. This empowerment is a source of energy that God created within you. You create the path your life will take by the choices you make along the way. This is a responsibility that your soul has chosen.

Many of you have forgotten how very powerful your thoughts and actions are within your own lives and the lives of others. What you focus on is drawn to you.

You all have your primary issues and your secondary issues. Your primary issues are the biggest ones in your lives, and the secondary issues are those that result from your belief systems and the patterns of the primary issues.

Throughout this book I will be talking about how your relationship with your parents has affected your life. Don't misunderstand me; I am not blaming your problems on your parents or caretakers. Some of you might appreciate them taking this responsibility, but you don't get off that easily.

You chose your issues for this lifetime. You will experience situations with these issues all through your life.

Those experiences only start with your relationship with your family of origin. You chose this family because their issues would coordinate with the issues of your life plan. The spirits of your parents, your siblings and yourself agreed prior to your birth that you would work together to provide each of you with the opportunity to experience and heal your chosen issues.

Your parents are playing their part in your life plan just as you are for them.

I will also talk about the importance of forgiving and healing your relationship with your family, whether they are alive or dead. Karma is created within any relationship, especially with those we love. It is important to heal as much karma in this lifetime as possible, or you will be back to experience it with them again in your next lifetime, and your next, depending on how long it takes you to learn.

You are your issues. These words are so true, as our life purpose is all about the growth and awareness that we achieve through the challenges of our issues.

Our entire lives are planned around these issues. Our souls are striving to evolve to the awareness of God and this is accomplished through the advancement and evolution of the soul.

As souls having the human experience, we must work through our many issues—experiencing them, learning about them and overcoming the negative aspects of these issues. This is how our spirit is meant to evolve. We are not asking you to stay focused on the negative aspects of your issues, but to have awareness of what you are creating so that the negative patterns can be transformed into positive patterns for the fulfillment of your life purpose.

Our lives are made up of relationships: whether these relationships are with family, friends or intimate partners, they are of great importance to the growth and awareness of your soul.

In your present situation you may be sabotaging your financial future by working in a job below your potential, or you may feel trapped in an unhappy relationship that is not meeting your needs, or you may just plain feel stuck in life. There is hope for the fulfillment of your dreams if you are ready to acknowledge the detrimental aspects of your life. Yes, it will involve change: change of your negative thought process, your negative beliefs and your negative actions. These are the factors that have created the situation you are currently experiencing.

ISSUES

We all have our primary issues and our secondary issues.

Our primary issues are the biggest ones in our lives, and the secondary issues result from the experiences, belief systems, and patterns of the primary issues.

You are given many issues from which to choose:

1. The **primary issues** include **Trust, Abandonment, Abuse, Control, Judgment, Responsibility and Love.**
2. The secondary issues include Anger, Patience, Forgiveness, Fear, Jealousy, Self Love, Self-worth, and many more which are experienced through the primary issues.
3. You may have chosen one or more of the primary issues, but each will connect you with other issues.

As you worked your way through your many lifetimes (yes, I have it on high authority that we have lived hundreds, some of us thousands of lifetimes), you will experience all of these issues.

Whether you choose to heal and overcome the negativity of an issue is up to you.

When you have healed a particular issue, you will no longer respond to an experience with that issue in the same way. The negative emotion that the issue once created for you will be diminished or it will no longer exist. Most of us work on the same issue for many lifetimes, often with the same souls.

How do we choose the souls with whom we will experience these issues?

It is actually through agreement. We belong to soul groups. Just as it sounds, these are groups of souls that travel through multiple lifetimes together, helping each other work on their issues. We trade off in the roles that we play with each other. The changing of gender, relationships roles, and ethnic groups is necessary to fully benefit from this opportunity we have been given for the evolution of our souls.

God did not expect us to accomplish this work by ourselves, so he gave us a support group and our soul group is only part of it. This means that it was through an agreement that you came into this life through your parents. They were chosen-your parents, siblings, children, friends, teachers and partners are all part of *your* life plan.

You have probably been with these other souls in many lifetimes, with roles reversed and altered to fit the needs of that lifetime. Many of you are thinking, "I couldn't possibly have chosen those parents or that child because look at the challenges they brought to my life." But, believe it or not, you did.

Your relationship with them was how you were to begin your experiences with your issues.

As a soul in human body, you could not experience the issues of abandonment, abuse or control if you came into a home of unconditional love and acceptance and then continued on to have a blessed life of peace and contentment.

That sounds like a great life, but how would you have the opportunity to experience those chosen issues in that particular family? This makes the experiences with our family, friends and teachers so very important. We have our initial experiences with our issues between conception/birth and adulthood.

So this means that our soul meticulously chooses our parents, siblings and surroundings very carefully, as they set the pattern for our entire life. There is no pressure here, as you have your support group assisting you with your life plan. This support group consists of Spirit, your personal spirit guides and angels, as well as your human soul group.

Your parents come into a lifetime with issues of their own, as every individual does. Their issues will interact with your issues giving each you the optimum opportunity for growth.

Imagine yourself as being part of a big puzzle, each piece connecting to the other, completing the whole picture. This is how you work with your soul group, each helping the other work through the experiences of their issues.

Remember, it's not always all about you! Before I understood this concept, I felt sure it was "all about me!" but not always in a positive way. My low self-worth caused me to blame myself for anything that went wrong, but I now understand that this attitude was inaccurate although it reflected my issue with judgment.

Sometimes when someone with whom you are interacting is projecting anger or judgment, you become a part of their lesson with an issue and the situation with their anger may not be about you at all. But the interaction gives you both the opportunity to process emotional memories previously created by the same issue but with others.

When I find myself angry and frustrated with someone, I must remind myself that it is my choice to hold onto the anger or release it and move forward with my life.

Have patience and search for a better understanding of what is really going on with you and the other person. Make conscious choices about how you are reacting. Before you jump to conclusions, figure out what part of the experience is yours and what part may be theirs.

It is just as important to help others in your soul group to heal as it is to heal your own issues. I understand that this change of perception is often difficult since life happens so fast that you typically react from habit. The changing of this habit has to be done on a conscious level with patience rather than with an attitude of judgment.

Every word, thought or action that you experience during your lifetime creates an energetic force. This energy is connected to an emotion, and you hold that energy within your body.

The love and nurturing that you receive from yourself and others feeds and nourishes your emotional bodies, to sustain you through your everyday life. But the negative energies created by your issues produce blockages that are held within your *chakra system* (energy centers within the body). Negative energies will create blockages in your energy flow that actually pull negative experiences or illness to you.

I have expanded more on *chakras* (pronounced *shock-rahs*) in Chapter Eleven of this book.

Our issues are first demonstrated in our childhood, but we experience them all the way through our lives. The issue(s) we chose to work on in this lifetime will keep surfacing to be experienced. These issues can create both positive and negative emotional memories.

These issues will be experienced in our childhood with our family, playmates, teachers and friends. As we become adults, we carry these issues into our relationships and then we wonder why we would choose someone to have a marital relationship with that is just like our father (for example).

It is your spirit that creates the opportunity for you to experience that particular issue through your relationships. This enables you to experience the emotions that are attached to that issue. These are the same emotions that this issue created when you were a child.

You will continue reacting in the same way, as this is the pattern that was developed from your original experience. Our belief systems are formed around the emotions experienced and perceptions of our childhood experiences. The energetic recordings of negative thoughts and emotions keep playing over and over in our heads. The words and actions of our previous experiences are so embedded in our soul that when we encounter a similar experience, the soul memory tape is activated.

We are controlled by our belief systems. These belief systems often become a blockage for our lives, preventing us from having the relationship or job that we desire. This blockage will also affect our happiness, our harmony and the balance for which we strive.

There are two sides to each issue.

Whatever issues you chose for this lifetime, you will have the opportunity to experience both sides of the issue in some way. For example, if your issue is abandonment, you could be the one that is abandoned and your fear of being abandoned could cause you to abandon others or to stay in a situation that is detrimental to your welfare in fear of being alone.

With the issue of abuse, you could be the abuser as well as the victim of abuse. All of your issues will be played out in this way.

The issue or issues on which you chose to work in each particular lifetime cannot be released from you. These issues are your purpose for being alive at this point in time.

They will be your issues throughout this lifetime, yet through working with these issues you will allow yourself to heal the karma attached to that issue. This will make life so much easier for you. This awareness gives you the choice of how you allow the experience with that issue to affect your life.

The following story may be an unusual analogy, but it explains the control your issues can have over your life.

Let's use your hand as an example. You are born with it, yet you never quite figure out how it works. However, it's a part of you and you come to accept it, but every once in a while your hand reaches up to slap you, painfully knocking you to the ground.

Although shocked by the situation that has been created, you still do not take the time to understand the purpose of your hand and why it keeps hurting you or to discover how you can make it more useful. By ignoring it, you enable it to keep repeating this same painful experience for you.

You eventually take on the belief that if this arm–that you love so much and depend upon for life–treats you in this way, then somehow you must deserve the treatment. You also begin to accept the slapping as something you have no power over, therefore allowing it to continue.

Try to understand how your issues might work in much the same way; the painful pattern of experiences that your issues create for you are often a mystery to you.

You see the same life experiences happening over and over again; yet you do not understand why this is happening. You feel powerless at stopping the repetition because you don't understand the cause.

Changing the outcome of the experience involves taking the time to get to know yourself better. By looking at your patterns, you can learn to identify your issues. Then you can learn to control your issues as well as learning to controlling your reactions to the situation that your issues create. Although the issue will never go away, you have the power to change the effects this issue has on you. **You can control your issue, or it can control you: this is your choice.** You can make the necessary changes to your life to determine how that issue affects you. Your reaction comes from the emotional memories that were created the first few times that you experienced the issue.

You have to acknowledge, understand, and release the emotion before you can heal your issue. A belief and a pattern were originally developed, causing you to recreate the same emotions or beliefs each time you experience that issue.

In this way, a soul chooses the issues that it will experience as opportunities for the growth and evolution of the soul. The issue of abuse, for example, can manifest in a physical, emotional or verbal way and connect itself to experiences with many other issues.

If a child receives abusive treatment from someone he trusts and loves, he takes on the negative energy of the action and the belief that he is bad and deserves the abuse. At this point, the child makes choices for his life. He may chose to become a bully, which enables him to make other children feel as worthless as he feels, or he can withdraw with feelings of failure.

In this way, secondary worthiness issues become connected to his experience, and the child will carry this **belief** into his future relationships.

Being the chosen issue, until this issue is understood and the emotions that are attached to the experience healed and thus are overcome, he will continue to put himself in abusive experiences with many different people throughout his life. The child believes that he is not worthy of love and acceptance, so consequently the adult accepts this as his truth.

This belief will also cause him to accept the abusive relationships that he unconsciously attracts to himself. All of this creates a **pattern** that he plays out with himself and in his other relationships. Even though this is done at a subconscious level, it nevertheless becomes a very powerful pattern in his life and difficult to overcome.

Here is an example of how our issues connect with our parents' issues and can percolate through many generations, continuing until someone changes the patterns. First, a soul chooses the issues of abandonment, abuse and judgment. This choice makes it necessary to have a family to play this out with, not as a punishment but as an opportunity to heal the soul's past experiences and change the negative beliefs for all involved.

Sometimes this may be a cultural pattern passed down through many generations. The parent demonstrates these actions, not understanding the damage it is doing to the family since it was part of their learned heritage.

The issues become embedded in the parent's personality.

Although not intending to damage the child's self-worth, the parent's actions of abuse (emotional or physical) and judgment create feelings of abandonment for the child. A perception of abandonment is experienced when the child does not have her emotional needs met, thus confirming her lack of worthiness.

Parenting skills are formulated from the example set by the parents, so each member of the family carries forward this lack of understanding in how to demonstrate positive love and a healthy feeling of self-worth. This lack of emotional support creates an insecurity that is often demonstrated through control and abuse. The parent-child relationship then creates experiences with the issues of abuse, control and judgment, so the patterns are established.

Whether the abuse comes as physical, emotional or verbal, it is still abuse. The child takes on the judgment that he is not worthy of love, believing that no matter what he does, he will never be good enough, and that he deserves to be abused.

It is not that the parent doesn't love the child, but the parent doesn't know how to show love and acceptance to the child in a way the child can identify. That child grows up with this example of love. As he becomes an adult, he then has the choice of continuing the pattern of abuse, control and judgment by treating others in the same way, or overcoming the examples demonstrated in this relationship.

As the adult goes through life, he will make himself miserable by subconsciously pushing away all those he cares about because he doesn't know how to give or receive love in a way that feels right to him.

This inability to demonstrate love becomes an emotional blockage for his life. Many times if we desire emotional support, we don't identify logical love as love. As a consequence, we create a feeling of sadness within us when our emotional heart is empty.

Even logically based people must eventually learn to show love in an emotional way, but it is often learned through someone they care deeply for and trust. This can be a spouse, child or friendship, but the opportunity will be presented to them as part of their human consciousness growth. This opportunity for growth is often achieved in the child-grandparent relationship.

When we lower the shield of protection that we typically hide behind, we allow ourselves to be in a vulnerable relationship. In this situation we are able to learn so much about giving and receiving love without judgment or fear of failure because a child loves unconditionally and responds with acceptance to all that it receives.

*This is only the case until the child hits puberty. Then all the rules are thrown out the window, life gets crazy, and the child begins creating major opportunities to play out his own issues, pushing all of the family's buttons as he begins his own journey in the challenges of adult relationships.

The other choice for the child with the issues of abandonment, abuse and judgment is that, as an adult, he may decide to stay in the "victim mode" by surrounding himself with people that treat him as if he has no value.

The child believes that no matter what he does, it will never be good enough, so he deserves the negative treatment that he receives.

In this case, the adult will put himself in a relationship with a mate who has the same controlling, abusive or judgmental traits as one of his parents. He may then go into a job where his boss has the same traits, and so again he is not valued or appreciated, no matter how well he performs his work. He has now achieved all that his limited worthiness beliefs allow.

This feels very comfortable to him since his self-worth tells him that this is what he deserves.

Again, remember that we attract these people to us so that we may experience and learn about our issues. This may feel like punishment, but it is not; it is the opportunity to free yourself from your negative beliefs.

You may wonder why someone would continue going down such a painful path. Often we go through many painful relationships and many demeaning jobs with the same pattern because these are the issues we choose for this lifetime and it is our purpose to experience them as an opportunity to overcome them. We learn about them through experiencing the lessons that accompany the issues.

The lessons come in many different forms, and that is why it is so hard to recognize them. That does not mean that you are condemned to stay in that negative relationship or in that demeaning job.

Do not misunderstand what I just said. Running from the situation is not the answer, as you will just recreate the problem in your next opportunity for a relationship or job.

It is helpful to understand the issue that created the challenge and change the belief that caused your response to the challenge. This knowledge and awareness changes the situation, empowering you to have control over the outcome of the situation. When you release the negative belief that has held you in the situation, you are then set free to explore all that you desire without the limitation of your belief.

Often we must continue creating these situations until we learn how to control the issue rather than letting the issue control us.

The spirit/soul of the person in the above illustration chose the issues of abuse, judgment and control. With these primary issues came the secondary issues of self-worth, love, anger, patience, fear and jealousy. This person also chose his family and everyone else in his life, agreeing that his family would be the first ones to activate his issues. These issues begin as the child is in the womb, because the spirit of that child has knowledge of what issues are chosen. As life begins, so do the experiences.

The blockages that I am referring to throughout this book are manifested within your life as negative beliefs.

These beliefs can have many forms that are often difficult to identify. This is one reason that they are so hard to change.

One such example is: The issue of judgment can be demonstrated as a negative belief about our worthiness to have something or someone in our lives. How many of you have demonstrated this belief in your life by subconsciously sabotaging a relationship or job?

In the case of a relationship, it is always difficult to overcome patterns that have been formed in your previous relationships. Until you deal with those painful emotions and memories, they remain ever present, often haunting your future relationships creating negative beliefs or patterns.

When you allow yourself to have a relationship you may find yourself tiptoeing through it, constantly watching for a sign that this person is going to hurt you in the same way as someone else did. This action of abandonment would be confirmation of your belief that you are not worthy of love. If this keeps happening to you in the same way, you justify the belief to be truth.

You may have created a situation in which you find yourself getting closer to a person when fear jumps up for you: the "What ifs?" start plaguing your life.

Before long you will allow your fear of being abandoned in a relationship to overcome your desire to be in the relationship, so you cause an argument in an attempt to push that person away, distancing yourself from what you fear might be eventual pain and abandonment.

That old belief that you are not worthy of unconditional love eventually destroys your opportunity to have a healthy relationship. You may not have even given the relationship a chance to work for you.

Maybe your beliefs were focused on a job opportunity that you had been wanting and even earned, but when the offer finally came, you sabotaged the situation because of your fear of failure or of being judged unworthy of the job. Your fear caused you to begin focusing on all of the bad points about the job to justify not taking a job that you deserved, or maybe an emotional conflict was created with your co-workers, causing management to question your ability to manage others.

If judgment has frequently been an issue for you, this situation may be common. You find yourself taking two steps forward and one step back, often causing you great frustration. You may be working at a job that is below your potential for fear of someone judging you of being unworthy of something better, or you have a fear of taking on the responsibility of a management position even though you are capable of doing the work. You are setting the intent for what you want and creating the situation. You enable these beliefs to sabotage your relationships, your finances, and your careers.

CHAPTER 3
THE CHILD WITHIN YOU

Your inner-child is an extremely important part of your soul's journey.

It is the part of the personality in which the experiences of your lifetime begin, proceeding into adolescence and continuing into adulthood. The inner-child holds the key to healing the issues of your current life. The inner-child is a part of your human consciousness.

The human consciousness is best described as your ego. This ego is the motivator of your life experiences and it works with your higher-self or spirit to assure that you fulfill your life purpose. There are many aspects to the ego, with the inner-child being just one.

The ego makes the choices that create the belief systems and negative patterns, yet there are many other parts to the ego. The ego is the perception that you create about yourself. It involves every thought, emotion and action surrounding your life. The ego is all about you.

Your joy, laughter, and playfulness resonate with the energy of your inner-child and this child exists within you, often trying to express herself and to be a part of your current life. The inner-child can also hold a great sadness or anger, depending on her experiences.

The energy and emotional memories of your childhood experiences are held within your inner-child. As adults, our reactions to situations are filtered through the emotional memories of our inner-child. This means that as an adult, when you encounter an experience similar to one that you experienced as a child, you will react according to the emotional memories of the child because a pattern has been established by that experience.

If you think about the people around you, you can identify the ones that still possess the twinkle in their eye of that inner-child's joy.

They may have a playful attitude with laughter and joy filling their lives, and then there are others who have put their inner-child away, afraid to be vulnerable because of their past experiences. They may appear to be more serious and protective of their feelings. This is often because of the pain and suffering that their inner-child experienced. The inner-child believes that if they are in control of the situation, they will not be hurt again. So the adult walks around with a shield of distrust for protection or to prevent anyone from getting close.

Without realizing it, we sometimes allow our inner-child to take over our lives and relationships. As a result, we might throw fits of anger, become selfish and mean, or we can become so afraid of being hurt or judged that we just hide from life. Although believed to be hidden away, this aspect of our personality holds a major level of control over the reactions we have to situations within our life. It is through this inner-child that we can heal the negative emotional memories that try to control our lives, preventing us from having the life that we desire.

Healing the inner-child is our key to finding happiness and fulfilling our life's dreams.

Spirit feels that counseling can be an extremely valuable tool for all of us. I have experienced the healing affects of counseling many times, but not always in a professional setting. I admit that there was a time in my life when I felt a professional counselor actually saved my life. Sometimes we are at the point at which only a professional counselor is able to get us to a place of healing, so do not disregard the value of their knowledge and experience. On the other hand, there have also been times when my personal healing has come from the open heart and the strong shoulder of a good friend willing to listen.

It is communication that we need most. Communication about our true feelings and emotions is important for the clarity of the whole picture.

Sometimes you don not realize what you are really feeling until you hear yourselves talking about a reaction to an experience or an emotion. Your guides and angels can bring you healing through messages which may be channeled through your family, friends or a counselor. Remember that your angels and guides will <u>never</u> give you negative thoughts or messages; they do not judge you, they only give you information to help you make the best decision possible. It is up to you to watch for their signs and listen to their messages.

This connection with your spirit guides and angels is best achieved through prayer and meditation.

Prayer is talking to God, while meditation is quieting the mind long enough to listen for guidance. You cannot receive the guidance of your spirit guides if you are not taking the time to quiet your life and your mind.

Often many of you do not go to God in prayer unless you are in big trouble or you are praying for others. Prayer is one way in which you can talk with your guides, but you can also have a direct conversation with them. They hear your thought; they know your needs often before you do.

Throughout each day you have many thoughts, but most of them are just mindless clutter. Meditation is like making an appointment with your guides to focus on your life and the direction you are going. I like to talk out loud to them so they are clear as to what I am asking of them, but that is not necessary.

Too often, clients come to me stating that they have had 10 to 15 years of counseling and still feel that they are not moving forward in their lives. Actually, the counseling had helped them to voice the pain of the adult patterns, enabling them to deal with their everyday experiences of life.

But what I have found through Spirit's work, is that the child's emotional memories actually cause the adult to keep repeating the same painful patterns. These patterns result from the child's belief system.

Therefore, to stop the negative patterns of your life, it is not the adult you need to heal—it is the child. **Your willingness to give your inner-child the love and nurturing that it deserves is the first step to loving yourself. Only when you love yourself will you feel worthy of receiving love from others.**

The inner-child holds the energy of the words, actions and emotions of all that it experienced. As a result, all negative energies must be healed and released so the adult does not continue to react from the negative emotional memories of the child.

The inner-child resides within you, and that child is controlling how you think and react to situations and people. Your inner-child is one of your most important attributes, since it is the key to your healing and was a part of you when you carefully chose the issues of this lifetime.

Some of the issues you chose include trust, abuse, abandonment, control, judgment, love, and responsibility just to name the big ones. Of course, these can be linked to issues with low self-worth, fear, patience, love, rejection, anger and forgiveness. These are tremendous emotions for a child to endure but that was the spirit's plan as it knew even before it was born what it would be experiencing in each lifetime.

Your issues began while you were still in the womb. Your issues, and even the family you would be born into, were all created through soul agreements.

The family, of course, includes the initial people in your life that activate your issues. As you passed through the womb, your human consciousness forgot the plan, but your spirit did not.

Knowing the plan, your spirit attracts to you the experiences necessary for your lessons. It is through your family experiences that emotional memories are created. Emotional memories are the emotions such as—but not limited to—joy, happiness, pride, fear, pain, anger or guilt that the child connects to a memory.

Each of these emotions has an energy connected to it. It is the negative emotional memories that must be released to rejuvenate the joy of the inner-child.

While some of your emotional memories may begin before birth, most start with the interaction between the child and the family or caregivers. Spirit has demonstrated for me, through our work with the inner-child, that the child will experience all of its chosen issues in some way between conception and approximately 16 years of age. Although in some cases, the spirit chooses to bring an issues into this lifetime from a unresolved previous lifetime experience and play out when triggered by a similar relationship.

Typically, issues will become interlinked with each other and their perceptions expanded as the child encounters more experiences. Our emotional memories are created through our experiences, and those emotional memories hold an energy of their own.

These same emotional memories will enable us to form belief systems, some of which are positive and fundamental to our growth. But the negative beliefs that we embrace about ourselves and our lives can create blockages for us. When the child expands its environment to include teachers and playmates, those issues will again come up, and more beliefs both negative and positive are formed.

As the child progresses into adolescence, experiences create more negative beliefs that flow into the adult life. These negative beliefs are blockages that cause us to get trapped in the same patterns.

I have found that the positive words and actions such as praise, hugs and kisses feed and nurture our soul. They produce an energy that sustains us in our daily life. This supporting energy motivates us to survive the challenges of life.

The giving of a hug is powerful; it is the sharing of your life-force energy. As humans, we all need these positive affirmations as confirmation of our worthiness.

Through my work with Spirit, I have discovered that the human ego works in unusual ways.

When a client's inner-child tells me about its memories, the inner-child quickly recalls the negative experiences of its life.

It has been my experience that the positive words, actions or experiences in their memories are usually focused around the holidays or times of celebration. The abuse from judgmental words and actions can become a negative energy that we can carry with us the rest of our lives. Even as an adult, words of criticism carry more power than words of praise.

This is an illustration you may have experienced: you have gotten a haircut or new hair style. When you leave the salon, you think it looks really good – at least up to the point when someone comments on how bad it looks and how you must be really upset about having such a bad haircut.

If your issue is judgment, or you are challenged with a diminished self-worth, that negative comment can hold tremendous power over you. Before that comment, you may have gotten many flattering compliments on your new hairstyle. But because of that one negative comment, you may become self-conscious and dwell only on the negative comment. Bam, there goes the self-esteem, deflated like a popped balloon. If, as an adult, negative words can have this powerful an effect on us, think how they can influence the self worth of a child!

The child's perception is often different from the adult's.

When I am working with adults and we are talking about a negative life experience, they are quick to say, "Oh yes, I experienced that, but I understand why it happened. And I have forgiven them for that." When working with Spirit or Abraham that response won't work if it is not really true, because through Spirit's assistance, I am able to see and talk to your inner-child.

If the pain has not been healed, that inner-child is quick to disagree with the adult ego, remembering vividly what was experienced and continues to hold onto the energy of the emotion.

The human aspect of the soul usually does not understand what issues it chose. Nor did the child understand what issues were causing his parents to treat him as they did. The child only knows what was experienced and the emotions he/she felt at the time. This is how belief systems are created and damage is done.

The belief system is made up of beliefs that the child holds about himself. They include:

- I am not worthy of love because my mother/father/care-giver does not show me love.
- I will always be a failure because no matter what I do it is not good enough.
- I am not smart enough, pretty enough, or strong enough to achieve success.
- Nobody has time for me because I am not important.
- I am shown criticism, anger and abuse because this is what I deserve.
- I am bad and people hurt me because that is what I deserve.
- It is ok for this person to hurt me because this is how they show me love.
- Love is not safe or secure.
- It is all my fault; I was bad so she/he left us.
- It is my responsibility to take care of others because they will value me if I do.
- My needs are not important, and if I express my needs, I am bad.

These are just a few of the negative beliefs the child can hold; there are many others. These beliefs are created from negative emotional memories. Those emotional memories are what we tap into to help heal the inner-child. I find that the adult has often placed the child, with all his emotional memories, in a pretty box, tied tightly with a ribbon and then placed on a high shelf in the back of their emotional closet, this action enabling the adult to avoid dealing with the emotions of their childhood memories.

To achieve the happiness, fulfillment, and success that the adult desires, the child must be healed. To heal both the adult and the child, we are required to let our inner-child out of the box and reconnect with that child, empowering that child to begin the healing process.

Since the higher-self or soul of the child chose the issues for this lifetime, those issues were part of the childhood experiences. It was also through our soul's agreement that the opportunity to address those issues would be with particular people from our soul group.

Karma is created and healed through our interpersonal experiences. Our lessons will bring us full circle with our karma. **The healing of the inner-child is done through self-love.**

This healing opportunity is part of the Grace of God, as his unconditional love and forgiveness of us, and our deeds is the example through which he demonstrates how to love. This example teaches us to have forgiveness of ourselves and others, and this is an important factor in the healing process.

The work with the inner-child and adult brings healing to the person or persons with whom karma has been created. But we must remember the child does not have the ability to understand or analyze any of this. The child only knows what it has experienced. Whether it was because of the abuse, abandonment or judgment, the child often believes that he is unworthy of love. This belief system totally dominates the child's perception of himself.

The child holds pain as a result of his experiences. If not healed, this pain is carried throughout the person's entire lifetime. This also applies to experiences with fear, judgment and anger, since they all are also attached to negative emotional memories.

So we must get in touch with that vulnerable child to assist him in the healing process. This healing can be done in many different ways.

The method I use starts by using vibrational energy to assist in the clearing and releasing of blocked energy in the *chakra system*-the healing process using my intuitive ability of connecting with your inner-child. Spirit gave me this very unusual way of healing the inner-child, and it has proven to be exceptionally powerful in bringing healing to my clients. Through this book we are going to share healing methods with you that you can implement in your life.

The inner-child may show itself in many forms: some are fragile and vulnerable; some are angry and resentful; others may be fearful and sad; while some are patiently waiting for acknowledgment, only hoping to be loved and accepted. Your inner-child needs you. This is your life and it is your responsibility to heal the pain of your inner-child so that you can fulfill your life purpose.

The healing process involves releasing of the negative emotional memories of the inner-child. Both the inner-child and the adult must participate in this healing work. This is a combined healing, as the adult supports and assists the inner-child while the inner-child works with its emotional memories.

Often we discover that the inner-child holds memories in vivid detail that the adult has blocked out. This missing memory is frequently the answer to why the adult cannot understand the beliefs or patterns that have been formed in his life.

The child must feel loved and protected to go through this healing process. It is an obstacle for the child, as it may feel powerless with no voice. It is important to empower the inner-child by listening and giving value to its emotions. God heals the inner-child and the adult with unconditional love. The inner-child and the adult must both feel worthy of receiving this love.

In Chapter Eleven of this book we will take you step-by-step through the healing process.

CHAPTER 4
THE ROLE OF BELIEF SYSTEMS

I have explained about the many different issues that each of you may have chosen for your life and how you interact with those in your soul group. If is detrimental to your souls evolvement to hold on to anger with the souls who agreed to share these experiences with you. On a spiritual level, your souls loved each other so much that you each agreed to come into this life to help with the advancement of your souls journey.

Your family members (which they often are) or spouses have issues of their own to resolve. Your purpose is to assist them on their paths of overcoming the negativity of their issues and they assist us. So what really happens in our relationships is that they push our issue buttons – and we push theirs.

The goal of this book is to show you how you can change your belief system, consequently changing the pattern of your experiences. We cannot change your issues, but we can help you change how you react to them, thus changing how you attract experiences with those issues to you. Through your relationship experiences you will be given the opportunity to heal karma from past life relationships as well as karma created in relationships of this lifetime.

As we experience our issues, emotional memories are formed. Through repeated experiences with these strong emotional memories, we establish our belief systems. The belief systems that you established during your childhood caused you to act or react in the same way with similar future experiences, eventually forming patterns. These patterns become blockages, preventing you from achieving happiness and success in relationships and career.

Your failure in achieving success and happiness furthers your belief that you are not worthy of achieving whatever you desire, so eventually you stop striving for happiness. Is this what you want for your life?

I thank Abraham that they have shown us that it does not have to be this way. We can take control of our lives! Knowing this gives us the power to do the healing necessary to make changes in our lives.

If you step back and observe your life, you may see the patterns of experiences that have formed.

We are often unconsciously attracted to a partner similar to one of our parents. Our parents were the first ones to help us experience the issues of our life path, but as we move away from them, we need someone else to keep these issues actively in our path until we have accomplished a healing of them. This is where our relationships come into play. I am grateful for relationships, since we would never have the opportunity to heal our issues without relationships.

Throughout the chapters on issues, I referred many times to belief systems. These are some of the belief systems that we carry; see if you recognize any of them in your life. I will go back and forth on gender but the beliefs are experienced by both genders equally.

"If I'm not perfect, who could love me?"

This type of belief is connected with the issues of judgment, love, abandonment and responsibility.

We acquire this belief as a child when we feel we have to earn love. Through the child's experiences, she is taught that she has to be the prettiest, smartest, or the best at whatever she does, to be valued. She believes she must earn love through perfection.

She sees this as her responsibility, to be the best, but her efforts are met with judgment and criticism. She soon feels like she is a failure, which causes her to feel unloved. No matter what she does, she never receives the love and acceptance that she so earnestly strives to attain. The child then judges herself as unworthy of love because she wasn't perfect.

As an adult she still feels that she has to be perfect to receive love.

Knowing she is not perfect, she has to create a shield to hide behind. This shield keeps anyone from getting too close to her and discovering the flawed person that she sees herself to be. She has an overwhelming fear that others will discover that she is not perfect and abandon her.

The shield protects her from being vulnerable, but it also makes her unable to receive the love others try to give. This confirms her belief that "I was not perfect, so who could love me?" The pattern she developed because of this belief sabotaged her relationships and pushed people away so that she would not be abandoned and hurt by them. She feared the responsibility of a relationship. When she didn't receive the love and acceptance as a child, she saw this failure as her fault.

Failing to meet the needs of her parents, to earn their love, she believed that she had failed to earn love before, and that she would only fail again.

As an adult, the belief and the shield had become such a deep-rooted part of her personality that she no longer noticed them, leaving her little or no understanding of why these patterns kept repeating in her life.

"I'm not worthy of having unconditional love."

This belief is connected with the issues of love, abuse, abandonment and control. When a child grows up in an abusive environment, all she knows is fear, anger and control. There is very little love to be found.

She yearns for gentle, nurturing, accepting love, but this is not the type of love she receives. In this situation unconditional love is nonexistent. She soon bases her worthiness to receive love upon her willingness to accept abuse. She grows to believe that she is not worthy of unconditional love, and that the emotion/action of love is typically associated with pain.

Armed with these beliefs, she proceeds into her adult relationships, looking for love.

Unfortunately, she is often attracted to a partner much like her abusive parent, someone who treats her with no respect or value. In the child's family experience she saw this treatment represented as love; thus the adult allows herself to accept abuse and control in the name of love.

The adult does not recognize this at first, because her perception of love is so tainted. Her need to be loved unconditionally blinds her to the reality. The abusive partner will profess love to her, but then he will turn around and use abuse and fear to control her.

This partner also recreates her issue of abandonment. She is afraid to leave him or cause him to leave her because she fears being left alone. Since being alone and unloved are her greatest fears, he plays right into her issues.

In her childhood, her self-worth and respect were stripped from her, leaving her feeling powerless. The pattern typically goes on from here. Many times the person with whom she has a relationship will eventually abandon her. By then, he has sucked the life from her, leaving her powerless and totally demeaned, causing her to be even more vulnerable in her next relationship.

All too often in her relentless search to be loved, she enters another relationship, but she is still influenced by her same negative belief system. She will then find someone who treats her in the same way and go right back into the same pattern, as this is what she feels she deserves.

This person certainly does not intentionally create the same type of relationship, as it is created on a subconscious level.

Abandonment, abuse, control and love—these are the issues she chose to experience.

Her spirit will keep attracting the same experiences over and over again until she has awareness of the pattern and learns to break it. Breaking the pattern is very empowering, but it is not easy to do.

The comforting part of this struggle is knowing that this healing is available to you. Your angels and guides will assist you when you are ready to reach out for help in healing your beliefs.

The beliefs in your life may not hold the trauma of the previous example, but they can be just as controlling in a different way.

"I am afraid to trust love or I will be abandoned."

Connected with the issues of trust, love and abandonment, this belief is difficult.

Just as the other issues originated in childhood, this one involves the child experiencing a great loss or disappointment. This belief is created from a fear. It often begins when a child experiences the death of a parent or loss of a parent through divorce. For the child, both occurrences are about abandonment.

As a child, we come into this world trusting that our parents will be there for us.

Our expectations are that our parents will meet our needs, whether emotional or physical. In the event of a death, the child suddenly has a gaping hole in his security net. This attaches fear and confusion to future security. The child feels the same fear, loss and grief that the remaining parent is experiencing. He feels that he has no control over the overwhelming emotions that surround him. All the child can identify are the emotions that he is experiencing at the time.

Another way that the child experiences abandonment involving his ability to trust love is through divorce. This can be very traumatic for a child.

The child may be caught in the middle of a painful custody battle, and he will be torn between whom or what to trust. In this case, the battle is waged over the child in the name of love, but it creates many negative emotions. Often the child is too young to understand what is really going on, but he knows what he feels. He connects all of the negative emotions of fear, anger and judgment with love and the pain that love can create.

Then there is the divorce in which one of the parents leaves the family unit.

To the child, having both parents in the home is a form of security. They see the action of the parent whom they love and trust leaving them as abandonment. The belief system about trusting love is established in a child's perception of this experience. That pain is ingrained into the child's emotional memories. These emotional memories create belief systems that go on to develop patterns. The belief is formed that they cannot trust love because it will bring them hurt or abandonment.

This belief system is carried through to the adult's life. It manifests in many ways, one of which is the shield or attitude that they project that keeps people from getting close enough to see their vulnerability or fear. Their personality is often perceived as unfriendly and distant, unapproachable or as having an attitude of superiority – all camouflaging their true emotions.

All of these methods can be used as a shield, to keep others from getting close enough to hurt them. We see this shield used in both friendships and interpersonal relationships.

Another way we may see our belief systems being demonstrated in our lives is when we sabotage our relationships through unnecessary confrontations.

When we begin to feel a close emotional bond developing or a strong attraction to someone, in our fear of being vulnerable, we push them away or abandon them before they can hurt us. Often we don't even realize why we are running.

In our hearts, we still hold the child's painful emotional memories and believe that we can't trust love. Even when we are in a safe, secure relationship; we maintain the wall of protection to prevent us from being too vulnerable.

During brief times of loneliness we will reach out in search of love or friendship, but our fear of abandonment is always lurking within us.

"I am not worthy of success or money."

This belief system is about judgment, control and responsibility. It can affect the manner in which we live our lives as well as how we succeed in our careers.

With this belief, we often take two steps forward and one step back in our careers. Our belief in ourselves and our abilities is established as children; what we are shown as children is the pattern we live by as an adult.

When the child grows up in a judgmental family, ruled by control and criticism, there is little room for motivation to improve, out of fear of failure.

The child has been given the belief that he is not capable or worthy of success. This belief creates a comfort zone in a world of insecurity where he puts himself in a job below his potential, with no opportunity for advancement. He will frequently find himself passing up opportunities to further his education or improve his ability to achieve success.

The mother or father may have struggled with success, causing the child to believe he must walk the same path. Often, if no one in his family had finished high school or gone on to college, he believes that an education is beyond his grasp. His respect for his parents' pride or cultural beliefs may even discourage him from achieving more. This belief frequently causes financial struggle.

Financial obstacles can originate from many different experiences. An example of this is that a female child is given the belief that women are not capable of managing money or being successful.

This is demonstrated to the child by the example of her father fully controlling the money decisions in the family. It is further established by the father's actions of judgment and lack of respect for the mother, creating the perception of diminished intelligence or value of the mother.

The female children learn that males are superior, and that the female is not worthy of success or managing money. This in turn creates the belief that a woman must have a dominant male figure in her life, believing that a relationship is necessary to have security. Since she believes that females are not capable of taking care of themselves, she will not pursue those roles she views as "for men only."

This belief can also be demonstrated in gay or lesbian relationships, when there is a dominant partner with male energy as opposed to a submissive partner with female energy.

Contrary to what we are often taught, all males do not have some superior talent for managing money—a myth that was created by the male gender to stay in control. This should take the pressure off of all you men out there that don't have the natural ability to manage money!

The issues of judgment are also attached to the belief that "I am not worthy of success or money," and it can be a blockage to both.

A client came to me asking for help in releasing her issue with money, complaining that money unexplainably ran through her fingers like water. We discovered the blockage was not only with money, but it also included success. As a child she was told that rich people were bad, and that they only had money because they stole it from others, which gave the child the concept that rich people were selfish and mean.

We could understand why she would be opposed to being selfish and mean, since this was her definition of success. Her father came from an impoverished family and worked very hard for his money. Her family rationalized their financial position by saying that rich people were selfish and mean.

When my client Maria was in a position of being very successful in her career and earning a large income, she found herself trying to dispose of it as quickly as possible. She was female, successful, and making money. Maria loved her job, yet she felt guilty and embarrassed to even have the money. We found that she was experiencing these beliefs based on what she had been taught.

Basically her belief was that if you had money you were greedy, selfish, and probably stole it from someone else. For Maria, we first had to discover where this thought was established in her belief system, what person or persons she associated the belief with, and begin the releasing process. (A version of this process is explained in Chapter 11)

Understanding the negative belief empowered Maria as she could then see why she had always felt like something had been pulling her backwards in her financial endeavors. This is just an example of how our unconscious judgment of success and money can block us.

Sometimes a belief system is deeply embedded into our thought process, but we do not realize that it is there.

Our lives may be sabotaged by the belief, yet we are unable to recognize it.

Whether you are male or female, if you are told that you are not smart enough to manage money, this will become part of your belief system. You may have the problem of money running through your fingers. You will feel that no matter how much you earn, your pockets are always empty. Even the examples that are set for us by our parents can affect how we manage our money as well as our lives.

If our parents were generous, we will be inclined to be generous. If they were frugal, we will have a tendency to be cautious with money.

What the child experiences and hears is interwoven into their belief system. Our mind is a very powerful tool, yet it only knows what it is taught and experiences. The child's mind does not have the maturity to fully understand the situation, and many beliefs originate from the child's perception of the situation and this perception becomes their reality.

Even as an adult, whatever you believe is reality for you, whether it is accurate or not.

If you believe yourself to be powerless, then you will remain powerless until you step out of that belief system and prove to yourself that you are powerful.

These are just a few of the belief systems we acquire and carry throughout our lives. I encourage you to look at your life and become aware of what belief systems are forming challenges for you and to consider how you can change these beliefs to better meet your needs.

CHAPTER 5
TRUST AND ABANDONMENT

TRUST

The issue of **trust** is truly the foundation for interpersonal relationships in life.

It has many aspects and is often associated with other issues, but it holds its own pain and blockages. Trust is the belief that someone is going to be consistent and truthful. It is knowing that you can depend on someone else to meet your needs–physical, emotional or security. Once trust is broken, a relationship is scarred and takes time to repair.

Trust begins at birth. An infant quickly learns whether the world is a safe place or not. If his cries are not comforted, and his basic needs are not met in a predictable way, the child perceives the world to be a place that cannot be trusted. As cries go unanswered, his attempts to reach out to others may stop. This results in a failure to properly attach to his caregivers.

Interactions with others do not seem beneficial, so the child may not learn how to engage in healthy relationships, resulting in fear of closeness, lack of impulse control, low frustration tolerance, and a lack of respect for authority. He will often continue to consider others as unpredictable.

- Your physical or emotional needs were not met as a child, so you
- can not trust others to value or meet those needs.
- You keep everyone at a distance and do everything for yourself, not trusting or depending on others.
- You do not trust that you are worthy of love. In past relationships you did not receive the type of love that you needed, so you feel that it must be your fault because you do not deserve love.
- You do not trust love, thus denying yourself the opportunity to receive it. Your experience with love in the past has been disappointing and full of pain, so you do not trust that others can fulfill your need for love.
- You do not trust people and their actions because in your childhood your parent(s) were deceptive with each other or with you, thus forming your belief that others can not be trusted to be truthful with you.
- You are very selective in your circle of friends, as they each have to earn your trust. Honesty is a major attribute of your friends, with little or no tolerance for deception.
- You do not trust yourself to make good decisions. You judged yourself and others for the failed relationship decisions you made in the past so you are very guarded in allowing yourself to form future relationships.
- You trust everyone with no discernment, causing you to continually be disappointed and hurt.
- You make excuses for people when they are dishonest with you, allowing them to continue treating you in the same way.

An example of the trust issues was demonstrated through the experience of Jill, one of my clients. She had the challenging experience of having two alcoholic parents. As many children of alcoholic parents do, Jill learned at an early age that she could not trust that her parents would be there for her. During most of her childhood, her parents disconnected themselves from their children, neglecting their basic emotional and physical needs.

Anger and abuse filled the household with fear. Jill was repeatedly disappointed and embarrassed by the actions and situations her parents demonstrated around her, which caused her to believe that in the future the people she loved would abandon her, betray her, and fail to meet her needs.

In the eyes of this young girl, if she could not trust her own parents to love and protect her, she then felt she could trust no one. Jill decided at a young age that she could only depend upon herself.

Because of her fear of trusting others, she created an energetic shield of protection around herself, not allowing anyone to get close.

Her childhood experiences formed a pattern that was to occur repeatedly in her adult life. Her shield accompanied her into relationships; behind this shield, she felt safe, but it was difficult for anyone to connect with her. She repeatedly gravitated toward men who violated her trust. In each relationship, she encountered some type of deception, betrayal, or abandonment. Jill was confused.

"Are all men like this?" she wondered, or was she really as unworthy of love as they made her feel.

In looking at most of Jill's past relationships, we found that she had been sabotaging the relationships herself by not allowing people to love her. She had abandoned her partners either physically or emotionally to prevent what she saw as inevitable hurt or disappointment.

Jill was unconsciously attracting men with issues very similar to hers as they had their own baggage of fear and insecurities. In their relationships neither party knew how to give or receive a trustful love.

Trust issues are often attached to many of the other issues, such as abandonment, betrayal, and abuse. Such relationships are very painful, but they are valuable opportunities to gain a greater understanding of the issue. Through Spirit's guidance, Jill was able to acknowledge the issue, feel the emotion, recognize the belief, and change the pattern.

Individuals have the ability to create the future experiences of their lives.

In Jill's case, through this spiritual guidance and healing, she was able to make the necessary changes to heal her life path and begin fulfilling her purpose for this lifetime.

Jane provides another example. The first time we did inner-child work, Jane and I were both surprised by what was revealed.

When I asked her to go back to the first memory she had of this lifetime, she began describing the darkness of the womb and she took us through the experience of her birth. She was consciously explaining to us her thoughts and emotions from the baby's perspective. For Jane, rejection and abandonment were emotional abuse as they created major trust issues with love. Here are her words:

When I was doing healing work with Linda, she inquired about doing inner-child work. I wasn't sure what it entailed, but I knew I wanted to start my healing process…. It was a rebirth experience – you know, where she takes you back to when you were born and what you remember from that time.

She began the relaxation part, I didn't think I would remember anything, but I soon started telling Linda about the darkness of where I was. I do not remember much about the womb, but I do remember coming out. It was very bright and very cold. I was carefully swooped up and swaddled.

At that point they turned me over onto my back, and I am looking up at my mother's face. She is smiling at me, but she will not hold me...I want her to hold me...I want her to touch me...I want her to hold me so close – just like in the womb...why won't she hold me...why does she just keep smiling?...it feels like I am beautiful, but from a distance – like she is admiring me...but not loving me...what is wrong with me?...okay, fine then.

I decided at that moment that I will have to take care of myself. I feel so alone – so abandoned. I did on that day, and I do to this day.

Following the birth memory, Jane recalled being rejected as a small child:

...That was only the beginning of my memories. Another vivid memory that came through was of being a small child standing in my crib crying out for attention. But my cries are not answered. The feeling of loneliness is overwhelming.... Why doesn't any one come?.... What is wrong with me?... Why don't they love me? I again feel unloved, rejected and abandoned.

As an adult, I have the belief that when someone gets mad or is unhappy that they will abandon me. My reaction is to take control and say, "Fine then. I will take care of myself," which in essence makes them go away because I push them away so they won't hurt or disappointment me.

I can still see that look on the baby's face, and it will make me cry if I think about it too long.

Jane's healing even took her to a past life:

...In another healing session with Linda, we were doing a past life regression. Linda took me back to a lifetime in which I recognized my current husband.

I could actually see myself in that lifetime. I saw my surroundings and even recognized people from this lifetime. What I was experiencing was during the medieval time. I clearly saw and felt everything that was going on around me. I saw myself with my husband (the same one from this lifetime).

What I discovered was that, if I kept pushing him away, he would go off with a harem of ladies, and there I was on the other side of the room that was very dark and I was all alone and withering away. I saw that I was creating the same abandonment then as I am now, in not accepting his love.

With Linda's help, I am learning to trust and receive love. I now understand how my fear of abandonment made me want to control everything in my life, even the way my husband demonstrated love.

Jane's early experiences of not receiving the love and acceptance that she wanted caused her to create the belief that love could not be trusted.

Having never received what <u>she</u> identified love to be - the emotional/physical love of being held and nurtured – she believed that she was unworthy of love. She had not been taught how to receive emotional/physical love.

She would often complain of the big hole in her heart that was filled with sadness. The feeling of sadness was because she would not allow herself to receive emotional love because the child believed she was not worthy of it.

This revelation was shocking to Jane: she had blamed her husband for not giving her the love she needed, when she had been the one pushing him away. Jane realized we had work to do as she now saw the healing that needed to take place within her, as well as her relationship.

ABANDONMENT

The issue of **abandonment** (rejection) can present itself as an emotion, an action, or a belief.

Abandonment can be created by someone physically not being there, or it can be experienced through the neglect of not receiving the attention, time or love that is needed.

A child may feel abandoned if a parent leaves them for an extended period of time. This could be if a parent has to leave them for out-of-town work or military service. The death of a loved one also creates the feeling of abandonment. A divorce can be particularly devastating to a child, since children do not understand why their life changes creating a separation of the family.

The child often feels responsible, believing they did something to cause the problem or did not deserve to be loved. Such experiences are demonstrated in one's self-esteem belief system. This demonstrates how we might begin our experiences with the issue of abandonment.

- When you experience the physical loss of someone you care about, you feel abandoned. This is demonstrated as both a physical and emotional abandonment. This could be the loss of a person to death, or the ending of a relationship; yet either way there is pain and grief over this loss in your life. You opened your heart and life to include this person, so the physical or emotional absence creates great pain.

- When you experience the loss of a job, you feel betrayed and abandoned by the company or the people that you trusted. Something as important to your future well-being has been taken from you, so you will need to work through a level of grief as you process this feeling of abandonment. Then you can move forward successfully into your next job.

- When you are in a relationship with someone who has become self-focused, you begin to feel neglected as your wants and needs are ignored. Your perception of distance from this person confirms your feeling of abandonment. This diminishes your self-worth as you begin to doubt your importance to have wants and needs.

- You can abandon yourself by always putting the needs of others before your own. This action demonstrates to yourself and others that you are not important and it is acceptable for them to treat you in this way.

- Abandonment is represented as a lack or absence of something in your life. This can be lack of health, money, love, friendship, acceptance or respect. Anytime that we sense emptiness within us, we are experiencing the feeling of abandonment in some form.

How has abandonment been demonstrated in your present life?

A client wrote the following narrative after we worked with her issue of abandonment. In her case, we worked with the "other side," the spirit of her deceased father. At first Sara didn't identify her issue as abandonment, but when we looked closer, this was what we found. Sara writes,

I have always thought of abandonment as a physical thing, I never gave much weight to the emotional aspect of it. I now feel that the emotional abandonment I felt as a child could be the core of many of the issues I have carried throughout my life.

From all appearances, my family looked just fine on the outside; everyone thought that we as a unit had it all together. Mom and Dad

were not divorced, two average, well disciplined children, home, cars in the garage, all the stuff that matters, but it was at times just a big shell of a family. My sister and I had all we needed, a nice home, food on the table, clothes on our back.

Sometimes I look back and the only feelings I have are empty, great big holes that I don't know what they are or from where they are coming.

My Dad, the great man he was to me, was very quiet and withdrawn compared to my Mom. Mom wore the pants in the family. Sometimes to this day, I still have resentment over that one.

Dad would come home every day from work (you could set your watch by the time he arrived home, same time everyday), he would always say his hellos, (we were not completely ignored, we did talk) take the Jack Daniels from the cabinet, fix a drink, retreat to his chair until dinner (we did at least eat dinner at the table as a family while we were young), back to his chair escaping through the TV until 9:30, then locked up the house and upstairs to get ready for bed. Yes, this was pretty much every night of my childhood best I can remember. Empty, nobody home is how it made me feel.

The most memorable talk I can remember having with my dad was when I was caught with drugs. I don't remember all the words, I just remember sitting on the floor in front of my dad watching him cry. I knew then that my dad was really human and cared for me more than I gave him credit.

My Mom was pretty much the same, but in a different way. Mom was a teacher, a very popular teacher and she had quite a following. I have no doubt that she changed the life of many children. Although, at times she seemed to forget about the two girls she had at home.

I always felt like I had to compete with the other children around her for her attention. Her emotions were pretty empty also, not that she didn't have any emotions, she just didn't know what to do with them.

Every day we would come home from school, my sister and I would do homework or go to play while Mom cooked dinner.

Then Dad would come home, the emptiness and almost fakeness of emotions would really turn into a play. After dinner Mom would usually either be on the phone with other kid's parents, PTA meetings, school board meetings, or something having to do with everything but us. Not to say she didn't do her part, she was always there to take us to our practices for whatever we were involved in at the time. She did help with homework, and as I grew older, helped me a tremendous amount with my music.

Still there was something missing. I call all this "the big white elephant sitting in the living room that no one knew how to handle."

I know my parents did the best with what tools they had been taught, but it led to some pretty explosive things in our family. These were things we would not be able to talk about if I had not gotten into recovery and brought those tools before my family. My sister and I looked to other things in order to fill the emotional void. I chose drugs and alcohol. After all, I saw my Dad come in every night and escape with alcohol. Why couldn't I?

My sister, on the other hand, was pregnant twice before she was 18. We both acted out in our own ways to get their attention, and as far as I felt, it only worked a little.

Through my work with Linda, I have discovered that abandonment is a funny thing— something that you feel but don't feel. Something that you see, but choose not to look at it. Something that is screaming at you to listen, and you walk further away.

Empty, that is the best way I know how to describe it. It was just a big hole in the soul that I was looking to fill in whatever way that I could. To do this you have to feel it, look at it and talk to it before you even know what this empty feeling is all about. You have to break the cycle of where it brought you, so as to make sure it doesn't follow you everywhere you go.

I discovered that this emptiness could not be filled by outside sources. This job was up to me because it involved loving myself before all else and I definitely had some obstacles to overcome.

Then my Dad died and things took a funny turn. I knew this feeling from somewhere, but didn't realize what it was. I just knew that it was empty and followed me everywhere I went.

Then suddenly the most beautiful thing happened. The spirit of my father and my spirit became connected in a way that I have never known. Linda enabled me to communicate with my Dad. Helping me to understand how he could be with me, and giving confirmation to my experiences. I was open and present to him and this time he was running to me with all this stuff, all of his love and dropped it all in my lap.

Even though he is not here, he is here. Even though I can't hear his voice, I hear his words. Even though I can't feel his touch, I am overwhelmed by his love.

I continue to struggle with the empty feelings of abandonment as they still need work and time but I have the best teacher of all– a father teaching his daughter how to start over again and look at things from a different light, the light of the Spirit.

This is just one example of how communicating with the other side enables us to heal issues with our loved ones even after death. Sara's experience is a great example of different types of love.

I will explain different types of love in future chapters, but Sara's parents expressed logical love that met the basic physical needs of their children. They worked very hard providing home, food, clothing and education, believing they were succeeding in demonstrating their love for their children. Sara and her sister, however, defined love as emotional love, and those needs were not being met. Because of their differences in definitions, Sara and Jennifer did not feel loved or nurtured; they felt neglected and abandoned. These were the issues they chose to experience and to heal. After Sara's father died, he returned to help her with the healing of her issues.

It was the child we had to heal before the adult could make changes to her life. This is an important fact in the healing process.

The inner-child is one of the keys to healing the emotional blockages of your life. In one lifetime there are many different aspects of who you are and your experiences. This one life is comprised of the childhood experiences, the adolescent experiences and the many different experiences of your adulthood as you have grown and changed throughout the years. It is the childhood experiences that most affect your belief system.

Even though you are no longer a child, you function with the emotional filter of the child's experiences. The energy of the emotions that the child had experienced is still an important part of who you are.

Those emotional memories unconsciously continue to affect your reactions when you encounter a similar experience or personality type. The child created a belief system that aligned with the child's perspective and emotional memories. This belief system is so integrated in the adult's actions and reactions that we are often unable to identify the problem with our actions.

In other words, we often find our angry, injured, five-year-old child driving our dream car down the major highway of life.

There are many aspects of the abandonment issue. Sue's story may enable you to understand another aspect of this primary issue.

When I worked with Sue, it was her inner-child that explained to us the emotional memories of her childhood.

Sue grew up in a military family. Her father was in the Air Force. As the military typically does, they moved numerous times and he was gone for long periods of time.

All the child knew was what she experienced. Because of the moving, her friends and playmates were continually left behind. Most of the time it was just the mother and the little girl doing the best they could, yet the mother had married young and really didn't know how to love and nurture a child.

Sue's father, the only male influence in her life, was very seldom there for her. Even when he was home, she couldn't seem to get the love and attention she needed from him. The short times he was around her, he didn't know what to do with a little girl. He didn't understand her emotional needs.

Consequently, no relationship was ever established between them; he was unavailable both physically and emotionally. He came from a family of little or no emotion and worked in an atmosphere of logic rather than emotion. It wasn't that he didn't love her, but, like her mother, he didn't know how to show it.

The child's perception of relationships was developed by what she experienced with her parents and the emotions created by the experience. These emotions created her belief system. Some of the issues she had chosen for this lifetime were abandonment and love. She believed herself to be unworthy of love or acceptance. Sue felt abandoned and rejected by her family, especially her father.

When Sue came to me, she was emotionally and physically exhausted. All of her *chakras (physical and emotional energy centers)* had shut down, and she had very little energy flowing through her.

Sue sat crying before me, unable to understand what had happened to her life. She felt that her life was in shambles, as she had gone through a string of failed relationships. We began by clearing and balancing her *chakras.* This was the first step to bringing her clarity and healing as it brings a sense of balance to the body.

Because of Sue's many failed relationships, she was no longer able to love herself; she desperately felt she had to find someone to love her. Her self-worth was so low that her own fears would sabotage any positive relationships.

Sue began believing herself to be unworthy of the love and acceptance she desired, she was so emotionally starved for love that she couldn't stop her obsession to have a man in her life; but she continued to reach out to men who were unable to love her in the way she needed.

Through Sue's interpersonal relationships, she was still reacting to the anger and pain that her inner-child felt.

As a child, she had not experienced love in the way that she felt she needed. Because of this, she had continually punished herself and the men in her relationships.

She subconsciously had been trying to change the relationship she had with her father by attracting the same type of person to her as a second chance, yet repeating the same outcome.

She didn't understand that her father loved her, but in his own way, which was a logical type of love. As the child, she was looking for emotional love. She needed the physical attention of being held and nurtured to feel loved. Since she saw these relationships as failures, she used them to diminish her self-worth.

Just as love is defined in different ways, so is nurturing.

The gesture of nurturing is typically defined as support and encouragement given to something or someone to grow, develop, thrive and to be successful.

In a healthy child-parent relationship, the child relies upon a parental figure to provide the nurturing factor. The lack or insufficiency of this action creates a trust issue for the child.

The logical personality type demonstrates this support through instruction and guidance, often believing that personal interaction is not necessary as their example is sufficient.

In contrast, the emotional personality type nurtures through a physical and emotionally interactive way. This can be shown through time spent together sharing hugs, thoughts and emotions. This type of nurturing is definitely a more interactive gesture. Your personality type determines the type of nurturing you need as well as the way in which you demonstrate your support for others.

This difference in definitions is often the unseen problem in relationships.

Abraham asked Sue to stop the torture she was creating for herself through these relationships.

They asked her to abstain from any more relationships until she healed her self-image. She had lost her self-worth and self-esteem. Since she did not love or respect herself, how could she expect others to love and respect her?

This was where Sue had to start the healing process. She had to work on releasing the beliefs of unworthiness that had been formed within her, creating patterns.

Sue identified the issue of trust as she felt that she could no longer trust herself to choose a positive relationship for her. We had to work with the inner-child to release the anger she had with her parents for not giving her the kind of love she needed.

She had to gain an understanding of her parents and their definition of love. Their love was a logical love, which is very different from emotional love. Sue had to love herself in an emotional way, accepting and nurturing the child within her so that she no longer felt unworthy of love.

Sue learned the many ways of receiving love without judgment and without the fear of being abandoned. Through Sue's healing, she now has a new vision of what her life can hold.

Although the work we have been doing with clients was aided by my gift of communicating with the inner-child and those in spirit, as well as energetically clearing the chakra system, we will share the knowledge and tools for you to do similar healing of your life.

In working with different clients, I began to realize how difficult abandonment was to recognize from the adult perspective, and how many of us have abandonment as one of our issues.

When Gloria came to me, we began by talking about her relationships.

When I asked her about her childhood, she said it was just a typical childhood with no unusual problems. I went on talking with Gloria about her life when Spirit gave me the word "abandonment."

I asked her where abandonment might be a part of her childhood. She denied experiencing it, as both of her parents were in the home. Her inner-child was quick to jump out and begin explaining to me that <u>she</u> did feel abandoned by her family and she was even madder that the adult Gloria was in denial of the child's pain.

When Gloria began looking at her childhood, she admitted that there was sadness. The child explained that her father came home at night, but the children were not allowed to speak to him as he would go into the den and hide behind the newspaper. He didn't give hugs and kisses, nor did he spend time with the children playing or talking. The child explained that she felt rejected and angry, and she also felt unimportant and not worthy of his love.

Gloria admitted that she was right and was surprised by this realization that her childhood **was** full of abandonment. The adult found herself uncomfortable even admitting that there were problems, for fear of judgment. She nervously laughed at all the emotions that began coming up within her.

We decided to do some inner-child work, allowing her inner-child to show us specific situations of her life that caused anger.

One such situation the child described in emotional detail. Gloria saw herself stranded at the top of a big tree that she had playfully climbed. She was only four years old, and she was very frightened.

She kept calling for her father, who was within sight, to come and help her. He refused to come help her and would just reply, "You got up there by yourself, so get down by yourself."

We tapped into all of the thoughts and emotions that the child was experiencing at that time. We saw the tears and terror, and finally the sadness and resolution that her father didn't care about her safety.

Gloria decided that she could not trust anyone to take care of her or to love her. She would have to depend on herself to get out of that tree just as she would have to take care of herself for the rest of her life. Much to her surprise, she was able to see the source of her beliefs that she was "not worthy of love and her emotional needs were not important."

The experience in that tree was only one of many experiences throughout her childhood that reinforced these beliefs.

If you look at this situation from the adult's logical perspective, you could see how the father may have felt that he was doing the best he could at providing the essentials for his family and this was his definition of love.

Yet the child needed attention and affection to feel loved. Gloria climbed the tree in an attempt to get her father's attention. His denial of attention was not about lack of love, he logically felt that he was teaching her a lesson and that she would be stronger from the experience.

His lack of knowledge about the child's needs is not unusual as they were two very different personality types that demonstrate love in different ways. Unfortunately this experience as well as many similar ones gave the child confirmation of her belief that she was not worthy of love or acceptance. She was also taught that she could not depend on others to meet her security needs.

We then discovered how Gloria's beliefs, associated with the abandonment issue, had created patterns throughout her life.

For instance, in her marriage and family she always had a problem trusting love. She didn't know how to receive love. Gloria's parents had been ill-equipped to teach her, so she did not know how to accept the love she was given by others.

She perceived love to be an action or situation that could not be trusted, so she created a shield of protection. Even though Gloria was surrounded by a loving husband and children, she still had an empty place within her heart because she didn't know how to receive their love.

Her inner-child instinctively knew the definition of love and how she needed this love to be demonstrated, but that place in the child's heart had never been filled.

As the adult, she would not allow herself to trust or receive love. This went back to her belief that she was not important enough to be worthy of love. These beliefs created many demonstrations of abandonment throughout her life. As we worked with her issues, Gloria explained to me that she had always felt people abandoned and betrayed her, when actually Gloria had created a pattern of sabotaging her friendships.

Her inner-child remembered the pain felt in her childhood relationships. To protect herself from the pain of feeling abandoned, betrayed or disappointed by the actions of others, she would push people away, often isolating herself as a way of protection. Although Gloria was now an adult, she continued to fear that she could not depend on others to meet her needs.

As we worked through the process of healing, she became afraid of the person she would be without the protective emotional shield. This is a common obstacle to healing. The thought of changing something is scary, even if the change is for your highest good. The separation that she had created from others and their love had become a comfort zone for her.

Gloria had become accustomed to what it felt like, even though it made her very unhappy and she did not feel loved, it was all she knew. Gloria realized her relationships would change.

The fear of opening up to be vulnerable in a relationship can overcome the need to be loved, especially if there is a self-worth issue.

The key to this is finding an intense love of self before trying to open your heart to others. Few of us are taught to truly love ourselves above and beyond anyone else, but this type of love is necessary for survival.

This may seem selfish, and we are taught that it is wrong to be self-centered. But to an extent it is necessary in this situation.

Logical people are often better at putting themselves and their needs first than emotional people because they have a survival instinct. That is one of the positive aspects of their personality type.

Emotional personality types can have so much compassion that they often meet the wants and needs of others before their own, depleting their source of energy. Depending on their issues, they often feel guilty for even asking to have their needs met.

The issues that you have chosen and the ways you are experiencing those issues will also determine your ability to show love to yourself. The manner in which you are showing love and respect to yourself demonstrates to others how you desire to be treated. If you are not protecting, nurturing and respecting yourself, then others will treat you in this same demeaning way.

The child that grows up without feeling loved in the way that it desires develops low self-worth and little or no self-love. Therefore the adult is unable to ask for love or accept love from those with whom he has relationships.

If you are able to step back and look at your beliefs and patterns, you are able to see what changes you need to make within yourself. This is done in an attempt at healing the old damage, to start making better choices about how you react to people and the situations in which you find yourself. The identification of these beliefs and patterns are the intent of the knowledge within this book.

Through the stories and descriptions of the issues, you will be able to identify your own issues as well as the issues of those with whom you have chosen to interact.

You may feel that you have overcome the challenges of your past relationships, but upon close examination, you may actually find that each relationship that you have experienced involves the same issues. They are just demonstrated in a slightly different way.

The determination of your advancement with an issue is proven by your reaction to similar situations. In examining the situation, what you will often find is a repetition of the same pattern and the same outcome – unless you consciously change your belief system. It is your responsibility to make this change.

Changing a habit or a belief is not easy, but if you desire it, there is hope for you to change the negative outcome of your present and future relationships.

At times, our expectations and perceptions of a situation cause the problem for our relationships. These are learned perceptions and expectations associated with the issue of judgment.

CHAPTER 6
ABUSE, CONTROL &
JUDGMENT

ABUSE

The issue of **Abuse** is difficult to describe because abuse can be **emotional, verbal, mental, physical, or sexual**.

While these can occur separately or in combination, each is very painful and damaging both to the child and ultimately to the adult's relationship with self and others.

Often the abused child becomes the abusive adult. It is a proven fact that abuse is often repeated through generations. We don't realize how abusive our actions can be, so we find ourselves continuing the patterns of treatment that we experienced. We suppress the pain of our childhood—these are the emotional memories that our inner-child holds.

The adult has forgotten how painful those words and actions were to the child. Sometimes the memories are intentionally stored away, but sometimes the memory is suppressed deep within the subconscious as a survival tool. This is often confusing for the adult, as he doesn't know the source of the pain or anger.

The adult may even observe his reaction to a situation and yet have no awareness of the source of his reaction. The abused child is taught that abusive treatment is an acceptable way of expressing himself, and the child did not have the knowledge to identify it as abuse.

If you were in an abusive family, you were taught to believe that this was how love was shown.

If not made aware of the difference, we continue to project abuse upon those we love. Depending on what your issues are, some of you may find yourself unconsciously drawing abusive treatment to you, while others of you may unconsciously or consciously be treating those you love in an abusive way. If you discover that abuse is your issue, it is important to understand that both the giving and receiving of abuse can be stopped and healed.

EMOTIONAL ABUSE

To explain the different aspects of abuse, I will start with **emotional abuse,** as this abuse can start while the child is still in the womb.

The baby (although I am going to call the child "he," I am referring to both genders) inside the womb has his own spirit. This spirit is so spiritually connected with his parents that he knows everything that both the mother and the father are feeling and thinking. The child senses if there is fear or anger around his existence.

If the pregnancy brings up negative emotions and reactions for the parents that continue throughout the pregnancy, the child will naturally feel unwanted. He then feels that he is not of value or worthy of being loved.

Without realizing it, the parents are already emotionally abusing their child, yet they do not understand their actions. If the child is unwanted, this emotional abuse continues throughout his childhood and may manifest as neglect. His needs for emotional and physical closeness go unmet. With emotional abuse, the child is often controlled through the emotional fear of abandonment. The child may be criticized for crying out and demeaned for expressing his needs. His biggest fears are used against him, as he feels punished by his parent through the withdrawal of love and attention.

Because his needs or desires are not met, he learns to suppress these needs, fearing that if he is too much trouble for the parents, they will be angry and not love him at all. This teaches the child that he is not important and that it is wrong to have needs or to express those needs. It also confirms for the child that it is acceptable for others to treat him in a disrespectful and hurtful way.

These beliefs, when played out in a relationship of any kind, are potentially detrimental to the wellbeing of the individual. Emotional abuse is typically demonstrated through the actions of an outside source, yet they can also be shown through the way we treat and value ourselves.

This type of abuse is demonstrated in our relationships through the demeaning emotional and physical interaction with others. A pattern of this treatment is established in our childhood through repetitive negative actions and words.

The perpetrator preys on the vulnerability of the child. A belief system is formed within the child that extends to his adult relationships. When the adult is in a situation in which he experiences the same feelings of vulnerability due to lack of security or love, this type of abuse is perceived as acceptable.

Abraham feels that the point about the child being spiritually connected with the parents is important information for all parents.

In the case of a parent choosing to give a child up for adoption: The spirit of the child has chosen to come into the world at that particular time and in that particular way. This is done through an agreement between the spirit of the child and the spirit of both parents. The child's spirit understands the choice the birth parents are making and has no judgment of it.

The spirit of the child is accepting of the decision as this may be the only way that this child can find his way into the appropriate family. Because the child takes on the emotions of the birth parents, it is important for the birth parents to express as much love and acceptance as possible to the child's spirit while in the womb.

This experience and the lessons of this experience for all parties involved is important and life changing. The child may have chosen the issue of abandonment and be experiencing it through the situation of his birth, but the birth parents can contribute to the healing of that issue through their connection prior to birth.

When adoptive parents are blessed with this child, they must understand that there may be an issue of emotional abuse to overcome as well as the issue of abandonment. Their availability to love the child is why this child chose to be a part of their family. There are never mistakes, but only opportunities for spiritual growth and healing. The spirit of the child and the spirit of the birth parents always stays connected as they are all part of the same soul group just helping each other fulfill their soul's purpose.

VERBAL ABUSE

Verbal abuse is often combined with emotional abuse.

The child is taught to believe that he is not worthy of love and acceptance when the child receives words of criticism and judgment. Words are very powerful tools that can affect a child tremendously.

Words used in any negative way, whether it be in anger, judgment, or control, are carried with the child throughout his life. The child's whole life may be affected by this negative self-perspective, causing blockages that will manifest and follow him throughout his life if not healed.

These blockages have the ability to manifest in many areas of his life. The negative words may come from family or teachers, as these are both figures to whom a child looks for reassurance of his worth and value.

An example of this was Mary and her hair. When I asked my client Mary what memories she had about her childhood, she pointed to her hair.

"I always hated my hair when I was a child because it represented my mother's anger with me," Mary told me.

When Mary was a child, she had thick, curly hair as she still does. Her mother was always irritated when having to comb through Mary's hair. Every morning when combing Mary's hair, her mother would gripe and complain with disgust about how unruly and difficult Mary's hair was. The child associated her hair with her value, and because of the words used and the energy behind the words, Mary felt that she was bad and unworthy of love.

Even though Mary was very smart and pretty, her life was spent hoping that no one would notice how ugly her hair was. Mary felt that because her mother hated her hair, everyone else would feel the same way.

Mary was always self-conscious, easily embarrassed and sensitive to the judgment of others. Words so thoughtlessly spoken by a mother to this child quickly corrupted the child's self-image. This belief was carried into the life and experiences of the adult. This belief system did not change for Mary until she was thirty-two years old.

Much to Mary's surprise, a man approached her in a restaurant one day, stating that he couldn't take his eyes off of her because of her strikingly beautiful hair and after having the pleasure of meeting her, that he would love to get to know her better.

Three years later Mary proudly became Jack's wife. It was only through the power of Jack's words that Mary was able to release the negative memories around her mother's words of judgment. Upon looking at Mary's life, we found how many of her mother's words of judgment had been wedged into her life.

She saw how those words and her beliefs had deterred her from living up to her potential, for fear of the negative judgment of others.

Mary's mother had no concept of the negative impact her thoughtless words of frustration had on Mary's entire life. She loved Mary very much, but she always looked for something to complain about, and Mary was the focus of her complaints much of the time.

Mary's adult self understood her mother and did not give her words much thought, but Mary did not realize how the child's emotional memories had been controlling how she felt about herself.

Here are some beliefs that are created through verbal or emotional abuse:

➤ **You are not smart enough**, so you should allow others to control your life and make decisions about your life.

➤ **You are not pretty enough**, so you should just settle for what is given to you and not have expectations of anything better.

➤ **You are not strong enough** to do something you desire. You are made to feel that you are weak of mind or body and you need someone to control your world.

➤ **No matter what you do, it is wrong**. You allow other people's negative judgment of you to determine your value or worth.

➤ **You will always be a failure.** These are like words of a curse that haunt your every endeavor, as failure becomes the expectation of yourself and your deeds.

A belief of diminished self-worth sets you up for failure because you eventually fear making an effort to try anything new.

➤ **Nothing you ever do is right.** What you did may have been right for you but not right for the person controlling your world. You live your life always trying to perform to someone else's standards. This automatically sets you up for failure because you have no control of their wants and needs.

➤ **Be quiet, you are too needy.** This demonstrates that the child/adult's wants and needs are not important. The child then fears that expression of their needs will cause the parent or others to abandon them or to stop loving them, if they are needy.

These are negative beliefs that have the potential of holding a tremendous amount of power over your life…but only if you allow them. You have the choice to determine who you are and what you believe.

MENTAL ABUSE

Mental abuse is connected with both emotional and verbal abuse, but it inflicts even more control and manipulation upon the life of the child.

The abuser takes control of how the child thinks about himself both physically and mentally, destroying the child's self-worth and self-love. It takes away the belief that the child deserves anything better than the abuse he is receiving, thus totally controlling and manipulating the mind of the child. This subtle form of abuse can be like a poison that eats away at a child and causes the individual to carry this energy and belief throughout his life.

PHYSICAL ABUSE

Physical abuse is about control, taking away the power and the will of the child. Physical abuse frequently occurs when the abuser feels he has no control in his own life and strikes out in anger, this resulting loss of control can be prompted by drugs, alcohol, anger or loss of patience.

Whatever the reason for the abuse, it still comes back to loss of control in the abuser's life. What it brings to the child is guilt and confusion.

The child takes on the belief that he is not loved, that he is not able to please the controller, and that he will always fail. He feels that if he is not worthy of love then he is of no value.

He feels that he will never deserve or achieve success in his life. He cultivates the belief that he deserves the physical abuse he receives, and he feels powerless to end it.

SEXUAL ABUSE

Sexual abuse can include the damage of all the previous abuses, or it can exist by itself.

The issues of control, trust, betrayal, self-worth and self-love are all connected to this form of abuse. It holds the negative emotions of pain, fear, anger, shame and guilt that damage a spirit and can be carried for a lifetime if not healed.

As with some of the other abuses, *sexual abuse* is about control. When a child is abused in this way, he sometimes does not remember the abuse until he is an adult. This does not mean that it doesn't affect him; this type of abuse can affect the child in devastating ways that others may not identify or understand. The emotional damage done to the child reveals itself in various ways throughout its life.

We experience all of our issues through interpersonal relationships, and this is especially true with the issue of sexual abuse. Because of the multiple levels of emotions attached to this experience, it is difficult to uncover all of the effects related to this type of abuse.

Whether consciously or unconsciously, the emotional memories create blockages that are played out in our other relationships. Without knowledge of the abuse, those around the child do not understand his eruptions of anger, withdrawal and fear. Nor do they understand why the child's personality changes so dramatically.

Hidden memories of this experience may be carried for decades. Such memories often come to the surface at a time when the adult is in a safe emotional time or place to heal. The timing of this memory is guided by the spirit of that person, as nothing is by accident, especially our healing opportunities.

The child does not always forget the action of sexual abuse. It is often connected to someone he loves and trusts. This emotional memory could be of the person he feels failed to protect him or of the person that actually abused him. Through his perpetrator's control, he is led to believe that this action is how he must earn love and value.

As the child endures the pain of betrayal, he is given the distorted image that this action is a demonstration of love. The child's perception of his self-worth and value is directly connected to his need to please this person that he loves and trusts.

The inner-child is extremely helpful when working with the issue of abuse.

When I do inner-child work, I channel an energy that relaxes the physical body and creates a sense of balance and openness. The chakra system then allows a releasing of any negative blockages within the physical or emotional body.

The mental piece of the process is similar to hypnosis, but the individual remembers the experience. I guide the individual in creating the necessary connection with their inner-child, that aspect of the individual will then begin guiding the adult through the memories of its childhood.

I am there to support the healing process as I take them through the steps of releasing and healing negative emotions. A connection is created between these two aspects of the individual as the adult will have strong thoughts and emotions associated with its childhood. The child's thoughts and emotions will be expressed through the adult. This part of the experience is often surprising for the individual.

Most often these are emotions that have been suppressed for most of their life. Because of the suppression, the adult is unable to understand or to identify where the negative beliefs originated. Reconnection with the inner-child is a very powerful tool in the healing process. In the workbook section of this book, I will demonstrate how you can use a similar tool for yourself.

The memories of Sylvia's issue with abuse were hidden deep within her soul for many years. There were other issues in her life that seemed to dominate her experiences but were actually connected to the pain of her abuse.

When Sylvia came to me, she recognized that she had a major issue with anger but didn't understand where its source. Her exact words were, "Life is continually pelting me with lemons and I was throwing them back at everyone in my life."

She felt she was surrounded with negative energy because bad things kept happening to her. She had gone through one difficult relationship after another. Every time a relationship started to get to the serious (intimate) part, she would sabotage it, but she couldn't understand why. She desperately wanted to be loved and to have a relationship.

She could not stay in a job for more than a year; she would either be fired or quit in a state of rage. Sylvia was a very intelligent woman with great career potential. There were many times throughout her life when Sylvia would find herself hiding in a bottle of whiskey to escape the trauma of living. Luckily, her need to support herself would draw her back to reality.

As Sylvia explained the drama of her life to me, I sat back and took a deep breath, for I knew what was coming. You have to understand that when I am channeling Spirit, of the two of us, I am often the more tactful one. Spirit wants you to move forward in your life, but first it is necessary for you to see that there is a problem and all of the details that surround this problem.

Gaining the knowledge and the understanding of the experiences of your life may be uncomfortable, or even painful. Spirit proceeded to peel back the layers of protection as we began to gently take Sylvia's life apart, patiently explaining which issues were creating her negative experiences.

Furthermore, she needed to understand that she had chosen those issues. I always hate saying that part, because I did not like hearing that about my life. Sylvia had chosen abandonment, abuse, control, trust and judgment. It was no wonder she was angry! That was a lot to deal with in one lifetime.

I saw the image of Sylvia's inner-child quietly appear beside her as we were talking. I am accustomed to the inner-child joining us for healing sessions with Spirit, so I smiled and acknowledged her to make her feel welcome.

After a while, as the inner-child began to trust me, she came to stand beside me. She told me that she had a secret that she wanted to share with me. I immediately knew what she was going to tell me. I had heard it all too often. The child told me about her father and her uncle molesting her for many years. She also told me that the adult had shut down all of the memories of the abuse.

I asked Sylvia about her childhood, and she replied that she curiously had very few memories of her childhood. I asked about holidays, and those memories were gone also. I wasn't about to present her with this newly discovered information—We don't work that way!

I did explain about the inner-child and how useful the child could be in our healing process. Sylvia agreed that she wanted to do the healing and I gave her homework to help her connect with her inner-child.

It took several sessions of allowing the inner-child to talk about her happy memories, as this allowed both the adult Sylvia and her inner-child to gain trust of each other. It was comforting for Sylvia to be reminded of the happy times.

The inner-child continued talking through Sylvia of memories, some of which Sylvia had prior memory of and some of which she didn't remember until the child guided her into the memory.

With Sylvia's eyes closed, she was able to see the experiences of her childhood. Sylvia was experiencing the emotions of the memories as they happened. I knew this work was preparing her for what was to come. We had actually tapped into a period of Sylvia's life that she had previously kept sealed shut.

In one session we saw the child at the age of five; she was frightened and told us so. She began describing a scene with great detail, allowing Sylvia to feel all the emotions. She painfully described in a small child's voice her experience of sexual molestation.

Sylvia squeezed her eyes closed tightly, not wanting to see her father's face, but she was deep into the experience of the memory. All of this was a complete surprise to Sylvia, but she could not deny it as she was a part of the memory.

Spirit stepped in at this point and began the healing process. Spirit's healing process involves the releasing of emotional memories and negative energy from the child, returning it to the person that created the energy.

Spirit then goes through a process of healing all parties involved with a healing energy and the Grace of God. After the session, she admitted that this revelation explained a lot of things that had happened throughout her life.

Over the next couple of months, we did a lot of healing with the many traumatic events the child had experienced. We released all of the hidden emotions that had been creating the anger within her. The adult had been sabotaging her life because of the guilt and anger the child held. She could not allow anyone to love her because she could not trust them.

The child felt she had no control over her life. This is where the anger emerged in her adult life as she used anger and intimidation to try to control others. This was also part of her abandonment issues, as she pushed both people and jobs away, believing she was unworthy of either.

What an experience we had in discovering the child's hidden emotional memories and how they were dramatically affecting her adult life. Sylvia went on to finish her healing, enabling her to take control of her reactions to future experiences produced by the same issues. The transformation in Sylvia was amazing as the carefree joy and glee of the child abounded. The child was released and healed, allowing Sylvia to receive love and happiness into her life.

The changes came quickly for Sylvia as she began setting goals and making plans to create the life that she now believes that she deserves. She is learning to love herself as she finds pride and joy in her accomplishments. It takes one step at a time to achieve the healing, but you have to love yourself enough to begin.

You may remember Gloria's story about her issue of abandonment by her father who would come home at night, go into the den, and hide behind the newspaper. What she had originally come to me with was her relationship with her mother.

Gloria acknowledged that she had a very strained relationship with her mother, and she resented the way her mother treated her. Gloria always felt that, no matter what she did, she could not please her mother. Because of her mother's unhappiness with her own life, she often struck out at others, including Gloria, but the child did not understand the action.

She defended her mother's actions by saying that her mother wasn't a bad person; this was just her way of expressing herself. Much to Gloria's surprise, her inner-child was quick to jump in and express her true emotional pain. Gloria's inner-child felt that her father had abandoned her daily, in leaving her with this woman who continually criticized, demeaned and controlled her children with her verbal abuse.

The inner-child was angry with both parents, as both had abandoned and betrayed her. She soon came to believe that this abuse was what she was worthy of in this lifetime.

It's true that the issues of abuse, abandonment, and trust were part of her chosen path. She was destined to attract experiences with these issues into her life until she healed them. Gloria had married a man who had many of the same traits as her mother. She had grown up with this negative expression of emotion, so situations immersed in this type of negativity felt comfortable, or at least acceptable. This is what she expected from love, because this controlling type of love was what she had always been shown in her relationships.

She still carried the shield, created by the child, to hide behind as her protection.

This shield created a wall between her and her husband, silencing any communication between them. Her husband had his own issues that were creating anger and depression.

Without communication, neither of them was able to help the other heal. Both were stuck in the darkness of the situation.

He loved her in his own unemotional way, and it worked for her because this was all she believed she deserved. At least, it worked for a while, until the weight of the burden of her unhappiness created such pain in her body that it got her attention.

Gloria was suffering excruciating pain in her shoulder and neck. Despite medications, therapy and acupuncture, the pain would not go away. The pain of her emotional memories had settled in her shoulder. For me, this was not an unusual symptom for suppressed emotional pain.

At this point in her life, Gloria knew something wasn't working for her and she needed help. Fortunately, as it usually happens, someone gave her my name. Her guides were hard at work searching for help as they knew that she was ready to heal her life. We worked through the process of healing the many different aspects of her painful emotional memories.

Gloria's story is an excellent illustration of how we can experience the energy created by several different issues in one relationship. Also, her story demonstrates the importance of soulmate relationships. We are strongly compelled to remain in soulmate relationships because they give us the opportunity to heal our issues as well as our soulmate's issues.

All of our beliefs will be carried from the childhood relationships into our adult relationships, continuing the issue of abuse. Emotional, mental, verbal, and sexual abuse may not leave visible marks, but their damage can last a lifetime.

The child comes into his parents' lives through agreement as his higher-self/spirit knows what issues he will experience. This knowing does not make the experience any easier for the human existence, but the spirit absolutely understands the importance of its life purpose, or none of us would choose to be born.

CONTROL

The issue of **Control** has two sides as do all the issues.

It can be a very powerful trait if used to improve and balance your life. But when control is exercised in combination with negative emotions and is forced on others, it becomes a very damaging experience.

Control is primarily about the fear of the unknown. As long as we feel that we have the situation or the person involved under control, then we are not in fear. When a fear of something originates, we strive for more control, and we may even reach out to abuse others with our need to control their lives. This gives us a false sense of power. When we feel powerful, there is nothing to fear. The issue of control, like abuse, is often an issue that is passed down through generations.

This issue may show itself in one or more of the following ways:

- You are overly protective (controlling) of yourself and your world. Your fear of not being safe denies you the experience of something new or the adventures in life.
- The more fearful you are of being in a relationship the more controlling you get.
- You learn to sabotage your relationships through your need to control their lives. It becomes a relationship tool.
- The more out of control your life is the more you want to control others.
- When you don't trust others to meet your needs, the more you feel that you need to be in control for your own security.
- Logical people like to be in control because that is part of their survivor skills.

- Being in control feels like organization and is perceived as safe.
- Being in control gives you a sense of power.
- Being in control can be demonstrated as suppression or security.

How is control being demonstrated in your present life?

I will use another example of control as it was demonstrated in Tim's life. Tim's father was a very powerful man in the community and well-respected for his "get it done" attitude.

His family loved him, but he kept them in a state of fear because his need to control everyone and everything became obsessive. Neither his wife nor his children dared disagree or even question him, in fear of his intimidating temper. He controlled people's lives through their fear of this temper.

Tim played the sports he was told by his father to play, but his father was never satisfied with Tim's performance, so praise was not something that Tim often heard. His father belittled the things that interested Tim and even the things in which he excelled.

Tim loved the sport of baseball, but hated playing it due to his father's constant criticism. This only caused Tim to feel like more of a failure. Tim was angry and resentful, feeling that he had never received love and acceptance from his father, only control and judgment.

In Tim's adult life, this perception created problems in making decisions. Tim had it in his mind that no matter what choices he made, they would be wrong and he would be a failure. Tim's lack of confidence and self-worth crippled his career.

Tim worked at a job below his potential for fear of failure. He accepted his manager's demeaning attitude, just making Tim feel worse about himself. Tim's belief that he would always be a failure created a pattern of unsuccessful jobs and unfinished projects, each confirming Tim's belief that he was a failure. Tim's lack of confidence and respect for himself drew him to a woman who totally controlled his life. It was a very unhappy marriage, but having someone else in control became Tim's comfort zone.

The belief system he took on as a child kept attracting the repeating experience of the same patterns. He accepted the emotionally abusive treatment from his wife, his coworkers and anyone else that wanted to dish it out. He became afraid to move forward for fear of the unknown.

Control is empowered by fear of the unknown. Tim chose this issue, but with healing, he did not have to keep repeating the same pattern.

Tim's healing was not easy. As some of us do, Tim got into his logical mode—and this energy healing stuff was foreign, unknown and definitely not logical to him!

But all of the information that came through from Spirit during our first appointment got his attention by explaining many of the events and people in his life. We ended the session by doing Reiki on him to open and clear his *chakra system* where he held all of the trapped emotions.

He hadn't been gone two hours when he called to make his next appointment. He couldn't figure out what had happened, but he felt more awake than he had in years and realized he needed more work. Although Tim was very unhappy, having someone else being in control of his life was his comfort zone.

He obviously feared the unknown. If he changed, how would his life change.? This was definitely a factor he needed to consider.

As our work progressed, I took Tim to a place where he connected with the emotions of the child within him. When he saw and felt the pain that his inner-child was still experiencing, he knew he had to be released and healed of his blockages to move forward with his life.

Tim told me how he surprisingly looked forward to our sessions with great anticipation. In these sessions, Tim gained a greater understanding of himself and his family as he learned to understand love. We worked through the pain and judgments, giving Tim back the confidence he needed to take control of his life. Tim made some major changes in himself and his life.

He even called to say he was playing baseball for the first time since he was a kid, and he loved it!

JUDGMENT

The issue of **Judgment** can obstruct one's life in many ways.

Like the other issues, it very seldom stands alone. Judgment can manifest itself as criticism, usually creating negative self-worth beliefs. There is a perceived level of separation that is created through judgment.

This perception can be experienced through self-judgment or judgment from another person. Such beliefs can jeopardize success in relationships as well as careers. For example:

- You allow the judgment of others to determine your worthiness to be loved.
- Your fear of judgment prevents you from applying for a better job or from taking a job more aligned with your potential.
- The judgment of yourself causes a low self-esteem, making you believe that you have to earn love.
- You judge others to be superior to you.
- You allow the judgment from others to become abusive for you.

- Negative judgment is often cruel and your judgment of others may be abusive to them.
- Your judgment of others creates a level of superiority that offends others, thus diminishing the quality of your friendships.
- Your judgment blocks you from receiving what you work so hard to attain.

How is judgment being demonstrated in your life?

We do things to achieve a level of success or satisfaction, but if our own negative judgment or the judgment of others denies us that feeling of satisfaction, we never achieve success. Consequently, you find yourself continuously going in a negative circle, seeking something that you don't actually believe yourself worthy of achieving.

When Paul first came to me, he had no idea what type of work I did. Someone had recommended me, telling him that he needed help and that I was very good at helping people when they were stuck. When I explained how I do my work, assisted by Spirit, he was truly skeptical. I wasn't sure he would continue.

But Spirit always knows what to do, and they way laid his skepticism by giving him some facts from his childhood that no one but Paul could have known.

While he was still somewhat skeptical, his curiosity got the best of him. As we began to talk about his career issues, we slipped quickly into his unhappiness with his entire life, including his relationships. Abraham was quick to begin explaining about issues and told him that his issues were abandonment, judgment, and control, just to name a few. He couldn't understand at first where all of these issues fit into his life, but he didn't run, so I felt this was a good sign.

As I helped Paul relax and connect with his inner-child, I asked him to tell me about his life. Paul explained how he'd grown up with a mother who was compulsive about a clean house as well as all other aspects of her family's life. His father could not endure Paul's mother's need for control, so he often escaped to his many projects. This left Paul alone to experience her sharp-tongued abuse, as he now calls it. Paul idolized his father and didn't realize the anger that his inner-child held about his father's abandonment, until we began our work.

Paul's inner-child was eager to join the healing process.

The child expressed anger at his father for leaving him to endure the mother's abuse. He felt unloved and unprotected by his father. Paul's child felt that his father wasn't there for him because there was something wrong with Paul. Paul even remembered his father's comment that Paul was going to be built like his mother, tall and skinny.

The boy was greatly hurt by the comment because he certainly did not want to be compared to his mother who was so abusive and critical, but the thought stuck with him. Paul also remembered back to a very young age the criticism he received in everything he did. He felt that to get his mother's love and acceptance, he must be perfect.

As we were talking, the inner-child gave a detailed account of an incident in which his mother told him to clean his room. Even at the age of five, he was well aware of her unyielding need for perfection. After spending hours preparing his room for his mother's inspection, he proudly presented it to her. The adult was experiencing the thoughts and emotions of the little boy as we watched the scene play out.

His mother entered the room, immediately finding fault with everything from the making of the bed to how the books were put on the shelves. When she was through with her criticism, she demanded that he stay in his room until it was done right.

Tears rolled down the adult's cheeks as the child spoke emotionally of feeling rejected, abandoned and unworthy of love. He had been reaching out to his mother, trying to meet her needs so that he could earn her love and acceptance. What he received instead was judgment, control and abandonment. Oddly enough, the child did not blame his mother for her reaction. He blamed himself, forming the belief that unless he was perfect he did not deserve his mother's love. Because of his negative beliefs, he would allow others to abuse him in future relationships.

The child talked about often hiding in his room, in fear of his mother's criticism because he didn't know how to please her. Her words of criticism were like knives that cut the child. He still carries those wounds today.

With his grades at school, only "A's" were tolerated. Anything lower was met with demeaning criticism. This judgment of his incompetence created such a fear of failure that he feared trying anything new. The words of criticism played so loud in his head that he had difficulty finishing any projects, feeling that they were not perfect enough to be appreciated.

In Paul's career, he doubted his abilities to the extent that he would turn down promotions in fear that he wasn't perfect enough. He expected others to hold him to the same impossibly strict standards that his mother had ingrained in him.

Paul's need for love and acceptance compelled him to pursue the "perfect" relationship. Upon examining Paul's relationship history, we began to see the pattern. Paul did not have the example of a healthy loving relationship. He had never been in a relationship in which he received love and acceptance for who he was. Paul had been taught that he had to **earn** love and acceptance. He saw his relationship as being dependent on his ability to be perfect. This was an overwhelming responsibility. He felt that anything that went wrong was his fault.

Instead of learning how to be in a relationship and working through the issues that would arise, he would run from what he saw as his failure.

He feared abandonment, but he created it repeatedly in his life, judging himself to be unworthy of love so that he continually pushed people away. His need for perfection created a control issue much like his mother's, making it hard for others to feel accepted by him. His belief that he must be perfect to be appreciated or loved was dominating his life.

It has taken a lot of inner-child releasing and forgiveness to help Paul heal.

Paul realized that he chose his issues of control, judgment, and abandonment to learn about love. Paul's relationship with his mother was difficult, to say the least—but he now understood that he had chosen her to help him with his issues. That type of relationship was necessary to help Paul attain a healthy perspective of his issues.

Paul's mother had loved him in her own way, meeting the basic needs of the child. This was how she had been taught to love and how she shared her love with others. Paul needed to learn how acceptance and forgiveness can be a part of a loving relationship.

Most important, he had to allow himself to receive that type of love from others and for himself. Unconditional love was a foreign concept to him. This type of healing does not occur overnight. It took a lot of work with the inner-child, as well as with the adult and his past relationships to achieve a healthy perspective of himself and relationships.

At times it is like someone turns on the light and you are suddenly emerge from the state of darkness that you have lived in your entire life.

CHAPTER 7
LOVE, RESPONSIBILITY AND ADDICTION

LOVE

We now come to the issue of **love**.

Love is not just an emotion. It is the root of our entire existence. The desire to be loved is what propels us through the challenges of our lives. Our need to experience love draws us to the relationships through which we will experience our issues.

Trust is the first issue we connect with love.

From the time of our birth, we are searching for love. As a baby, love is having our needs met, both physical and emotional. When these needs are met, we identify this sense of security with the feeling that we are loved.

Next, we determine if we can trust that love. Can we depend on the parent or caregiver to continue meeting our needs? This is how trust is connected with love.

Love can also be attached to all of the other issues. The way in which a person receives love as a child determines the child's belief of his worthiness. This in turn affects the belief of the adult's worthiness to receive love.

A child's spirit comes from the arms of God, knowing only unconditional love. The child comes into this life with the anticipation and the expectation of receiving this type of love from his parents. Unconditional love is an unending love given without judgment or obligation. It is given without restraint, and is not something to be earned.

If the child does not experience this type of unconditional love, he feels abandoned, eventually believing that he is not worthy of love.

If love is presented or perceived as control and abuse, the child connects fear and pain with love, thus feeling that he is not safe and needs to create a wall of protection. If this situation is repeated, a belief system is established and no matter who tries to express love to the child/adult, the love is not trusted and therefore cannot penetrate the wall of protection.

Because of our instinctive need to be loved, we feel that without another person's love we are of no value. This creates a frustrating circle of negative energy. What most of us do not understand is that it is the love of self that is most important, but frequently we stop loving and valuing ourselves because of our own belief systems.

We may not be able to identify love with words, but when the emptiness within our heart is filled, we recognize the energy of love. Without self-love, we allow ourselves to experience loneliness or abuse in the search for love.

As a child, we experience the example of a loving relationship through the experiences of our interfamily relationships. In other words, what the child receives in the name of love is how he will frequently define love throughout his life—unless he is taught differently.

Love is a very powerful tool. The abundance of love can empower us to deal with the biggest challenges of our lives and to conquer them. We will go to battle, risking our lives to defend those we love as well as fighting for their love. The energy of love can create a feeling of elation with which no drug can compete. Through love, we receive praise, recognition and acceptance. Whether these come from self or others, it is still love.

Love can be romantic, secure, comforting, trusting, emotional, or physical, just to name a few of its many aspects.

Love creates a relationship that allows us to experience our issues of trust, abuse, abandonment, control, and judgment. It will also create the emotions of anger, fear, patience, jealousy, and forgiveness. The experience of love can destroy our self-worth or it can inflate it.

We instinctively base our value on the power of love.

Without the love of others, we often feel our lives are not worth living. When we are not receiving love, we judge ourselves to be of no value, eventually losing respect and love for ourselves. (When taken to the extreme, this is sadly the point that some reach, causing them to destroy their lives through suicide.)

The negative experiences we have with love as a child cause us to create shields to protect ourselves. These shields are created by fear—a fear that enables us to be hurt through abandonment, rejection, abuse, or betrayal. These shields keep us from trusting others to meet our need for love.

Our self-worth then tells us that we are not worthy to receive love. We use all of these fears to create the shield to protect ourselves from the pain of love. This belief will also cause us to push people away, denying ourselves the fulfillment of a loving relationship.

Sometimes, in the name of love, we allow people to use and abuse us. Our need to be loved is so great that we create the illusion of love in a relationship that in reality provides no love at all.

I would like to share Alice's experience with you. Alice's parents divorced when she was eight years old. She was passed around between various family members, having little or no security.

When we talked about her life as a child, she really could not remember feeling love from anyone in her family. Her grandfather had sexually molested her from the time she was eight until she was twelve years of age. Anger, fear and abuse were part of the everyday emotional experience of her life. When she was sixteen years old, she met Joe.

Joe was the first boy to show her any real attention, so she quickly fell in love with him. They made grand plans for their future. They married when they were both eighteen years old and soon started a family.

Joe was a hard worker, so they always had a roof over their heads and food on the table. He took the responsibility for his family very seriously. But just like her father, Joe had a bad temper and demonstrated it often. Alice kept telling me how much Joe loved her and the kids and how hard he worked to provide for them.

She accepted the treatment of being demeaned, abused and controlled because this was how she was used to being treated. She loved Joe because he gave her the security that she never experienced as a child. She tolerated his treating her with abuse in fear that he would abandon her and the children. She remembered the fear and insecurity with which she had grown up and she did not want that for her children.

When Alice came to me, she was suicidal. She didn't know what she wanted. She just knew that she was miserable and hated her life, and she was beating herself up with the guilt stick for not appreciating her life because her husband "loved" her and took good care of her.

After listening to her describe her life and family, we explained to Alice that although her husband was meeting her security needs, she was under the illusion that love was only security. Her spirit knew better. Its need to be nurtured was in starvation mode!

Since neither physical security nor emotional nurturing was part of her childhood experience, she didn't have the full perception of what love should be.

Alice had always been under the illusion that security was enough for her. She also felt that control and abuse was her husband's way of showing her love. When I asked her to define her needs, she was not capable of identifying them. As I explained to her what emotional needs were, we discovered that not only had it never occurred to her that she had emotional needs, but she also realized that there had never been anyone in her life who had tried to meet those needs.

She had totally lost her own identity trying to earn the love of others. To avoid dealing with her own emotional starvation, she threw all of her energy into taking care of others. This was why she was so unhappy with her life. She was starved for emotional love. Her spirit felt she had abandoned it and its need to be loved.

She neither loved nor respected herself because of the abuse she had endured. Her illusion of love was no longer enough for her.

This deficiency of emotional love in the relationship was not entirely her husband's fault.

Neither Alice, nor Joe, had learned through their childhood experiences about meeting the emotional needs of love. Alice knew that something was missing in her life, but she could not identify it.

Alice and Joe's spirits had united them in this relationship to learn about love, but neither had an instruction book. Because of Alice's history and her low feelings of self-worth, she did not realize what her emotional needs were, leaving her unable to express them to Joe. He was oblivious to any problems, just thinking she had become extremely moody.

Joe was repeating in his relationship what he had experienced while growing up. Joe was taking care of the financial responsibilities of his family, so in his eyes he was showing them love. He didn't realize that there was any other kind of love. Because of Alice's childhood history, she had never felt powerful enough to set boundaries as to how she needed to be treated; this was part of her lesson with Joe.

In working with clients, I recognize that while the relationship appears to be the obvious problem, I work to heal the root of the problem, the individual.

In Alice and Joe's situation, we had to heal the child so that the adult could find the self-love that she had lost in her childhood.

Alice had chosen the relationship with Joe to give her the opportunity to work on the issues she had chosen for this lifetime. Those issues were abuse, abandonment, control, trust and love. She needed to heal the emotions of the issues that had been created in her childhood.

The beliefs that she had taken on as a child were creating blockages for her. These blockages were making things so painful for her that she was forced to make changes in her life. Alice's underlying anger and frustration had created a blockage of energy in her shoulder and neck, causing continual pain. Pain makes us pay attention to issues that we would otherwise ignore. (This is Spirit's way of nudging us.)

Alice had to rediscover her self-love and identify her emotional needs. This did not happen overnight, as you may imagine. However, I am proud to say she is getting there and having a great time with the adventure. She now has a completely different definition of love.

Joe is challenged by the work and still doesn't know what to think about me, but he loves Alice enough to keep trying. They could not have stayed together if Joe had not been willing to learn about his wife's need for emotional love, as well as making major changes in himself.

Louise Hay has written several books about healing the body that I highly recommend. They may help you understand how energy blockages are created in the body and manifest as pain, illness or disease. This information not only gives you a better understanding of how the body works, but also how to heal it.

Communication is an essential part of any relationship.

Imagine with me, if you will, that you speak only English and that you are in a relationship with someone who speaks only French. No matter how much you love one another, you will encounter a tremendous amount of confusion and misunderstandings when you do not communicate in the same language. We find this same lack of communication in many relationships as people do not know how to express their needs to one another.

It will take persistence and patience as each one struggles to understand the wants and needs of the other.

I have found it to be a lot easier to love someone if you can understand who they are and what they are about. You no longer have to try to read their minds or assume you know what they want.

As you learn to speak one another's language, you gain a better understanding of how **you** can show love in a way that your loved one can receive it and vise versa. This knowledge makes communication in a relationship much easier, and communication is essential, whether it is between partners, family, co-workers, or friends.

When we gain knowledge of the issues that each individual brings into a relationship, we have a place to start on the healing of that individual. As the individual is healed, we can then make an informed choice as what to do about the relationship.

Each relationship that you experience has great importance to your soul's journey.

The purpose of that relationship is to give you the opportunity to experience your issues, make choices as to how you will react in a given situation and proceed with a greater awareness of who you are and what your needs are.

Each relationship that you have combines different issues to be played out as an opportunity for personal growth. Have you ever noticed how different people have a way of pushing buttons for you and you are totally surprised or unprepared for your reaction, later wondering what had happened and why you were set off in that way.

From a perspective of awareness, what really happened was that your two spirits agreed to the interaction in an attempt to give you both the opportunity to experience an issue and heal the negative emotion attached to the issue. It is your choice to determine how many experiences you need for the completion of the lesson.

RESPONSIBILITY

Responsibility is the last (but not least!) of the primary issues.

When we choose this issue, as the others, do it pairs up with many of the other issues. Just as the other issues can be connected to past lives, so can responsibility.

In the previous story about Joe and Alice, Joe's definition of love was demonstrated through being responsible. He showed his love for his family by meeting all their basic needs of food, clothing, and shelter.

In Joe's family, responsibility was a very important trait and was significant in how his family showed love. The emotional demonstration of love was very foreign to Joe. So when he had a family, meeting the financial responsibility and basic outward needs of his family was his way of demonstrating his love.

If you have the issue of responsibility, you may come into this life feeling an overwhelming responsibility to take care of others. We see this as a positive trait in doctors, nurses, and healers of all kinds. They willingly take on the responsibility of doing for others, whether it is taking care of family or strangers in a financial way or physical way. If their issue is responsibility, they are compelled to do this. This is also how they determine their value as they are doing for others.

This issue started for one of my clients when she was a child. Karen, had always been referred to by her family as "the server." While growing up, Karen hated the term, but as she matured, she found pride in it. Here is her story:

I came to see Linda for the first time in 1999. As my story unfolded over the next few years, I came to realize that I had made the decision to come back to earth with an overabundance of challenges. I chose to be born into a family riddled with alcoholism, sexual abuse by a family "uncle," emotional, mental, and physical abuse by a rageful and often drunken father, and spent most of my childhood frightened by a brother and a male cousin who took great delight in locking me in closets, tying me up under the bed, and generally terrorizing me just for fun.

My entire family referred to me as the "server." The boys would let me play with them only when I would agree to do whatever they wanted. I referred to myself as a prisoner of a childhood war and I was subservient to everyone in the family.

My family life was totally dysfunctional. I became an early alcoholic and felt that I could only change my reality with alcohol. I suffered from low self-esteem and had frequent anxiety attacks.

I chose a number of ill-fated marriages, had several affairs, gave birth to two sons, adopted one daughter, buried still-born twins, suffered through two miscarriages, my step-father raped me, and my oldest son went blind from a rare eye disease at the age of seven.

All this was fodder for drinking. I had no problem-solving skills and no spiritual belief system for sustenance. I had yet to experience love, trust, or peace.

In 1986, I discovered my youngest son was embarking on a journey of drinking and drugging. Terrified that he would die, I sent him to a six weeks' treatment center. During the "family week," it finally came to my attention that I came from generations of dysfunctional people rooted in alcoholism, anger, fear, resentment, and betrayal, and that I had unwittingly passed it on to my children.

I became absolutely desperate to find solutions and I followed the advice of the professionals at the treatment center and began a program of recovery. As the months went by, I watched my son improve. He came to believe in a power greater than himself, he forgave me for my shortcomings and became a wonderful person who turned his life into serving others.

As he changed, I knew I wanted what he had. Gratefully, I eventually discovered that I, too, was alcoholic and began to embrace the program of Alcoholics Anonymous.

Over the next few years, I began seeing a psychiatrist who specialized in post-traumatic stress disorder and alcoholism. With the help of therapy and medication, my anxiety subsided and with great difficulty I managed to focus on the twelve step program of AA, which brought me much relief, but to my dismay, was not the total answer.

My relationship with my father never improved. It was always combative and his second wife, Jo, didn't like me. In the summer of 1993, my father wrote me a letter telling me that he was going to sever all relations with me because Jo didn't want to be around me. But in December of that year, she had a massive heart attack.

My niece called about the event. I had a battle in my head trying to decide if I should try to contact him or not. My heart said yes and my ego said no. The next morning, I awoke to a vision or a dream (I'm not sure which) of Jo standing at the end of my bed. The only thing she said was, "Forgiveness is the Answer." Then she disappeared.

There was no doubt in my mind that spirit had sent me a message. I immediately called Tucson and spoke with my father. He tearfully asked me to come. Several family members also rose to the occasion and Jo died a few days later. I would say that we made a small amount of progress, not perfection, in repairing our relationship. We were more civil and polite to each other than anything.

I continued with the psychiatrist, went to recovery meetings, read every self-help book available, and took my medications, but something was still missing. My self-esteem was still questionable, my relations with my family of origin were still tenuous, and I was still struggling. Then a very good friend recommended that I visit with Linda Drake.

From the moment I met with Linda, I knew that this was going to be a key piece to my life's puzzle. My healing sessions with Linda put into perspective my quest to release and forgive my perpetrators while forgiving myself for my actions with my children.

Slowly, Linda and Spirit showed me how to work through the rage and fear and doubt and sadness and my inability to love myself. Through her amazing energy and spirit work, my heart began to open and allow me to realize that I chose this life for my own reasons.

My willingness to forgive my family was tested in 2000 when my brother was dying of cancer. He ended up living with his daughter, my niece, about 100 miles from my home.

She had two small children and for six months, I drove there one day a week to try to assist her. He hated me coming. He didn't like me and was very vocal about telling me that he didn't need me and I was way too bubbly for his taste. I did a considerable amount of praying before I would go through the door at my niece's home and I learned to speak to him in a calm voice and assure him that I was there for his daughter. He was so verbally abusive that I would cry all the way home. But I knew in my heart I was doing the right thing.

I would go to Linda and we would do healing and forgiveness exercises and I would return to his side. After three months of his relentless abuse, he growled at me, "Why do you keep coming here?" I quietly replied, "Because I want us to find for-giveness and healing before it's too late." He turned his head to look at me and with tears in his eyes he growled, "Well, see… it's happening now."

From that day on he still growled a bit, but he stopped the abuse and acted like he was glad when I came. He would tell me of the spirits around him that were waiting and how glad he was that they were there. After a life-long relationship of mis-trust and hatred, my brother died in July 2000, and I carry the knowledge that our years together on earth were not a mistake but an opportunity for learning.

Had it not been for my work with Linda, this healing would not have taken place. Nor would the mending and forgiveness of my parents.

A year after my brother died, my mother's health took a nose dive. She was unable to take care of herself anymore, she was mostly alone and supposedly she had but a few months to live. So I moved her into my home. Not surprisingly, she thrived with my children and grandchildren visiting on a regular basis.

Except for once when she was angry and referred to me as the "server," we got along very well. I had to set boundaries for any name-calling and thereafter we enjoyed each other's company. She was quick and witty, enjoyed my friends and the special attention she received. She stepped in and out of the doorway of death for the next three years as she struggled with her lung disease.

When I was a child I thought of her as weak because she did not protect me or herself. My perceptions changed as I saw her strength, her ability to forgive and ask forgiveness. She knew she had not been a perfect parent, but she did the best she could.

Eighteen months after Mom moved in with me, my father was diagnosed with lung cancer and other related breathing problems. He too came to reside in an assisted living facility close to me. So I had both of them. He was still surly, angry and argumentative, but with Linda's help, I made a decision to let go of my need to be right and I stopped fighting with him.

During the next year, I took care of him as best I could. He finally told me that he loved me and that "I had turned out pretty good." What a miracle. Spending this time with my father gave us the opportunity to heal our relationship. During his end-of-life journey, it was my ability to "serve" and his need to be cared for that gave us the opportunity to find the love and acceptance we had each been searching for.

Our relationship was taken to a new level as I discovered that in many ways I was a great deal like him. His failures had been my failures. His beliefs were my beliefs. His actions were my actions. And Jo was right. Forgiveness was the answer. He passed in December of 2004.

Shortly after the new year of 2005, Mom's health began to decline at a rapid rate. Only four months later, she passed.

I have no regrets for spending the time and energy on the people who I once hated and regarded as perpetrators. I found love and forgiveness in my heart. With Linda's help, I received one of the most sacred blessings on earth. And, yes, I "served" these people.

Because my son's visual impairment, I have been an advocate for the blind and visually impaired for more than 30 years. I feel that it was another opportunity given to me by God so that I could understand how my need to be the "server" changed the lives of others. I understand that I chose a life of service and being the "server" with a loving heart is my truest and most valued gift.

I understand now that my parents were supposed to be my parents, my brother was not an accident and my son is blind for a reason. And through working with Linda, I understand that I am who I am supposed to be. How I fulfill my life purpose is up to me.

In working with the healing of Karen's life, we used many different methods of healing. Spirit guided my actions and words as they created the opportunity for Karen's healing. We always started out with the clearing and releasing of negative energy from the chakra system. We then proceeded to work with Karen's inner-child, going back to the source of the emotional memories.

We have found this interaction with the emotions of the inner-child to be an essential part of the healing. Through this process, we enabled Karen to heal many of the emotions and beliefs that had created the blockages in her subsequent relationships. Her life held one negative pattern after another. We worked with releasing, going step by step through all of the major relationships in her life. (This process is similar to the one that I teach at the back of this book) We then proceeded to work with Karen's self-worth issues.

Karen's spirit had chosen all seven of the major issues for this lifetime and her inability to have a healthy relationship demonstrated how her issues were actively manipulating her life.

In examining her relationships, Karen found that most of the men she had attracted to her life had many of the same traits as her father. Her father had no respect for women as he emotionally abused them with his judgment and control, going on to physically abuse Karen's entire family each time he came home drunk.

Throughout Karen's childhood she was aware of her father's womanizing and his threats to abandon his family if they did not meet his measurement of perfection. Despite all of the negativity that Karen's father inflicted on her family, Karen just wanted her father's love and acceptance, always feeling that it was her responsibility to make him happy and feeling that if he wasn't happy with the situation it must be her fault.

Karen's diminished self-worth convinced her that what she deserved in this dysfunctional relationship and treatment became Karen's pattern of what a relationship should look and feel like. The negative aspects of the family relationship created Karen's definition of love.

When Karen began forming her own relationships she also worked from the detrimental pattern of her childhood beliefs. Of course, the relationships did not appear to be detrimental in the beginning, but she would soon find herself in love with a man who was deceitful, abusive, controlling, judgmental and unable to give her the love she desired.

This pattern became Karen's expectation of men and relationships. Karen was creating her own destiny.

Karen's addiction to alcohol aided in the destructive behavior that seemed to be ruling her life. Why had Karen been attracting men so similar to her father? Prior to coming into this lifetime, Karen had actually chosen the issues that she had been experiencing through her relationship with her father.

She specifically chose her father because he had the same issues that she did and he was the perfect person to create the situations from which she would learn. When Karen became an adult and was able to leave her family situation, her lessons with those issues were not over.

Part of her purpose was to learn about overcoming the negativity surrounding her issues, so she subconsciously attracted the same type of men to her in order to provide this opportunity.

Unfortunately Karen had never learned to love and respect herself, so she did not know how to teach others how to love her in this way. The combination of Karen's drinking and her diminished self-worth created one challenging relationship after another. Karen could no longer trust her own choices; every time she reached out to be loved, she would either be hurt or abandoned by the love that she desired so much.

In each of her relationships her belief that she was not worthy of love was confirmed and she learned to put up her shield of protection so she could not be hurt. As much as Karen had been hurt by her father's actions, his traits began to emerge in her relationships but through her actions this time.

Because of Karen's drinking, her fear of not having control in her life made her even more compelled to control other people's lives. Her chain of painful experiences made her suspicious and judgmental, yet the heart of the child just wanted to be loved, making her very vulnerable in her relationships.

Karen chose the alcohol in an effort to escape from the pain of her childhood, but her addiction took over her life. The alcohol became Karen's biggest lesson about control. She did not want to take responsibility for her life or what she was creating because she was afraid of failure. She just went from one disastrous relationship to another searching for the missing part of her.

In our work we found the missing part of Karen to be self-love. Karen had never been taught to love and value herself because her life had always been about taking care of others.

Karen had been taught that she had to earn love and someone else had the right to determine whether she was worthy of love by their acceptance. When Karen began her life of sobriety, she was taking her most important step to loving herself, but she soon discovered that she had many more steps to go.

By working with the knowledge of Karen's issues, we gained a better understanding of the choices she had made for her life path.

She discovered why she had attracted certain people into her life and what they had come to teach her. This knowledge not only brought her a tremendous healing of the past, but also empowered her to take control of her life as well as helping her to make more informed choices for her future.

The issue of Responsibility can also be connected to commitment. Many people have a pattern of running from a relationship if it begins to get serious or involved. This stems from their fear of commitment.

Commitment to a relationship is accepting the responsibility of meeting the needs of someone you love as well as your own. Whether physical or emotional, relationships involve a great deal of responsibility. Those people with commitment fears are afraid they will fail themselves or others. This fear can become a blockage that prevents them from having a mutual loving relationship.

I frequently find the fear of responsibility experienced by couples when they are preparing for parenthood.

One or both of the prospective parents may have a conscious or unconscious fear of parenthood. They fear of being like their parents and failing their children. They may maintain the belief established in their childhood that they are not worthy of love nor are they worthy of the responsibility of caring for a child.

When we discover where the fear originates, we are able to heal the responsibility issue. This changes our reactions to our experiences.

The responsibility of parenthood is tremendous! Often I work with women who chose abortion early in their lives and are having difficulty getting pregnant again. We find this is connected with the belief that they previously failed in their responsibility as mothers, and they Subconsciously judge themselves as being unworthy of that responsibility again. Through our healings, we have assisted in the growth of many families.

I will share with you a delightful story. Carmen and her partner decided they were ready to start their family. After trying unsuccessfully for a long period of time, they decided to pursue alternative healing methods. Carmen came to me and we discussed the problem, Spirit began to explain that the problem went back to Carmen's birth. We began with inner-child work to relive the event.

At the time of Carmen's conception, her mother was young and unhappy. She had two children already, and she certainly did not want another. Even in the womb, the baby Carmen knew this, and anticipating her challenge of her upcoming life, Carmen was very frightened. The delivery was difficult for Carmen's mother and she almost died in childbirth. In our regression, Carmen saw and felt the emotions of the baby as it was being born: feeling afraid, rejected, and abandoned as she was quickly taken away to the nursery. The child did not understand the separation, only feeling more abandonment.

We saw through the child's eyes that there was no motherly love or nurturing at her birth or in her childhood to follow.

Carmen's mother continually blamed the trauma of the birth on Carmen, using her as a scapegoat, making the child responsible for everything that went wrong in the mother's life. Others in the family followed the pattern, treating her in the same mentally/emotionally abusive way.

You may be able to understand the subconscious fear that the adult Carmen held—the fear that the birth of her child would hold the same trauma. Through our work we also found Carmen's fear of the responsibility of being a parent.

Because of her mother's abusive example, Carmen feared being like her mother. The abuse in her childhood caused her to have little or no confidence in herself; this had created blockages throughout her life, sabotaging many of her relationships.

It was only when these blockages deprived her partner (someone she loved dearly) from happiness, that she was motivated to heal her longtime pain and fear. This healing changed her life in many ways; teaching her to love and value herself as well as how to receive love from others. The great news is that Carmen now has two beautiful twin boys and she has proven to herself that she can break the negative patterns and beliefs that were created in her childhood. She has also learned to trust the love that her partner and her children give her.

The responsibility issue can create co-dependency in a relationship. This happened to Charles, who always saw himself as a knight in shining armor. But by the time he came to me, his armor was pretty beat up!

As our sessions began, Charles explained that he came from a family of five children. His father worked long hours to support the family and his mother's health was very frail. Charles, being the oldest, took on the responsibility of caring for both his mother and the younger children. Charles described himself as driven, as he remembered working to exhaustion while making many sacrifices. He didn't remember having a childhood, as he was forced to grow up very early to meet his family responsibilities.

Spirit explained that Charles derived his self-worth from his success at meeting the needs of others. One of his major issues was responsibility.

The belief he had established was that he had to earn love by taking care of others, this belief created patterns that Charles carried into his relationships. Charles' first two marriages were full of struggle and he was totally confused about why they didn't work. He believed that he had given his best, but somehow they were never happy with what he offered and he always felt as if he had failed both himself and them.

In his first relationship, Charles found himself deeply in love with Julie, the most beautiful woman he had ever seen. Her beauty was only exceeded by her insecurity, as she clung to him in desperation. Of course, this made him feel great, the knight in shining armor saving her life.

He was again working with his issue of responsibility and earning love. In reality, her insecurity became an illness. He was soon to discover that she was schizophrenic, and she became uncontrollably violent. He desperately hung on to this relationship for several years, allowing his issue of responsibility to override the reality of the situation. In this relationship, Charles experienced his issues with abandonment, abuse, control, judgment, responsibility and love.

Abandonment was one of Charles' greatest fears, so for a long period of time he would not even consider leaving Julie. Because of Julie's illness she was extremely abusive, both emotionally and physically with Charles, or at least Charles used her illness as the excuse for her actions and he allowed her to continue acting out in that way.

As the relationship progressed, Julie's control and judgment diminished Charles' self-worth to the point that he hated his life and who he had become. But his need to be loved and his responsibility issue held him bound to the relationship.

His angels must have been working hard trying to save Charles from the experience his own issues had created for him. Charles explained how devastated he initially felt when in a fit of anger Julie had thrown him out of the house. Although feeling as if he had just been set free from prison, he still carried the guilt that he had somehow failed her as well as himself.

Charles determined his value based on the happiness of others. He had never learned to love himself and to meet his own needs.

Believing himself to be unworthy of love, Charles avoided relationships for several years. After the pain of the last one, he preferred being alone. This worked well until Amy literally fell into his lap. They laughed about the experience. Through their daily interaction as co-workers, they soon became friends. She began sharing her financial problems that were compounded by health issues. Here came that knight is shining armor again!

Charles began by loaning Amy money and giving her advice about her financial situation. Feeling really good about being needed again carried him right back into the responsibility role. The attraction quickly turned to love, and he soon found himself in another marriage.

As Charles had turned Amy's life around by fulfilling all of her needs, he had rescued the wounded bird, earning her love thus boosting his self-worth. This marriage lasted for several years while he nurtured her through an illness, teaching her to be strong and confident. He shared all of his strengths with her, but because of the failure of his first marriage his fear of abandonment caused him to become overly protective to the point of suffocating her.

The more self-sufficient she became, the tighter he gripped her. He needed to feel responsible for her, as well as her being reliant on him to confirm his self-worth and worthiness to be loved. The control that Julie has used over Charles in his first marriage became the very tool that he was using to destroy his second marriage. Despite his love for Amy, he could not accept her growth. Charles' judgment of himself continued to control his life because he feared that as Amy expanded her world, there would be no need for him in her life.

The suffocation finally became too much for her. He had transformed the image she had of herself and given her the confidence to take control of her life. Now it was time for the wounded bird to fly away.

He again saw this as a failure since he had lost something that he dearly loved. The experiences with his responsibility issue had brought Charles many challenges, but he still failed to understand the problem with his relationships. In our healing sessions, we had to work with the inner-child since the child didn't feel loved for who he was, but only for the work he did in taking responsibility for others.

This caretaking was how he earned love from others as well as himself. He only valued himself when he was serving others. We found the inner-child to be very angry that his childhood had been sacrificed in meeting the needs of others. He felt unloved and unappreciated for those sacrifices.

He held anger at his parents for the situation and then guilt for being angry.

Charles prided himself on his strength and composure. He was surprised at the emotional tears that flowed from the inner-child as he began to express his true feelings. He began to see the reality that he had always met the needs of others while disregarding his own emotional or physical needs. He had failed to love and value himself for who he was rather than what he could do for others.

As Charles learned to love himself, he realized that it was his responsibility to meet his own needs and not to look to others for confirmation of his value.

The issue of **responsibility** can also hinder success in our careers. Often we cannot pinpoint the origination of an issue in this lifetime, but when we look to a past life, we find the root of the problem.

This was Sam's experience with his issue of responsibility at work. Sam realized that he had sabotaged many jobs in the past when it was time for advancement. He would create problems and then blame his frustration on the job, his boss or co-workers, inevitably not seeing his own fear. Sam finally recognized the fear, but didn't understand it.

The time had now come that he was being offered a management position after working for a company for many years. It was a great opportunity. He knew he could do the work, so that was not the problem. But he had an overwhelming fear of this responsibility.

Sam had been told about me, and he figured it was worth a try, even though he was very skeptical.

When I explained about past life regression, he was eager to discover his blockage. As we began the regression, Sam's spirit guides quickly took us to the lifetime that was connected to this particular issue. Strangely enough, I could see it, but Sam could not. He just stood in darkness. When I asked Spirit what the problem was, they told me that Sam was afraid to see the truth.

Spirit assisted me in helping Sam to release his fears, and we quickly proceeded. Sam began telling me about the people he saw around him, the clarity of their dress and familiarity amazed him.

As we probed deeper into his experiences of that lifetime, we discovered many things, but the significant part came at the end of that life. We learned that prior to the stock market crash in 1929, Sam had been running a large investment corporation belonging to his family.

When the stock market crashed, he lost everything that his family and clients had worked to acquire. He felt that he had failed not only his family, but the many clients who had trusted their savings to him. This failure of his responsibility was so devastating and overwhelming that he committed suicide.

In this lifetime Sam's fear of failure had limited his job opportunities to those far below his potential while creating financial struggle within his life. Sam did not understand why no matter how much money he had, it was never enough to cover his bills. We discovered that subconsciously Sam felt such guilt at losing others peoples' money in his previous lifetime that he felt that he did not deserve money in this life time. Sam saw his current life as a failure, and he feared the responsibility of creating the same experience of failure when managing others. His survival instinct of this lifetime brought forth a fear in him that also blocked him from creating the same life-ending experience.

After working with that particular past lifetime, we were able to release his fear of responsibility, and the past life regression gave him an enlightened view of other issues in his life. Through knowledge we can obtain healing.

When we place the responsibility of our lives and happiness totally in the hands of others, we have no control over their choices. When we take responsibility for our own lives, there is nothing to fear because through our choices, we make our lives what we want them to be.

If you have the issue of responsibility, you may come into this life feeling an overwhelming responsibility to take care of others. We see this as a positive trait in doctors, nurses and healers of all types. They willingly take on the responsibility of doing for others and this may be demonstrated by taking care of family or strangers in a financial way or a physical way.

If their issue is responsibility, they are compelled to care for others. This can also be how they determine their own value as well as how they see others valuing them. The issue of responsibility is also demonstrated in "the protector." The police officer, fireman, and military personnel fall into this category as they feel great pride and self-worth in the protection of others. It is their responsibility issue that makes them so good at what they do.

This issue maybe demonstrated with one of these beliefs:

- I am responsible for the happiness of others. This belief can be a trap when we put the happiness of others before our own happiness.
- I am financially responsible for others. This belief can be a trap as we sometimes enable others to not take responsibility for their lives by doing too much for them.
- I take responsibly for negative outcomes even when it isn't my fault.
- I am responsible for others so I must control their lives to keep them safe.
- I fear responsibility so I avoid making commitments to relationships and/or jobs.
- My fear of responsibility allows others to control and abuse me.

- I give others the responsibility for my happiness and well-being.
- I do not want to take responsibility for my actions so I blame others for anything that goes wrong.

What beliefs about responsibility do you hold? How are these beliefs contributing to your life?

ADDICTIONS

I will preface this portion by saying that I am not a licensed therapist and have no formal education in this area. I work with Spirit, channeling their knowledge and healing. If you have an addiction of any kind, I highly recommend you seek help from a qualified professional!

I have to include addictions with issues, as addictions can manifest experiences with all of the issues. Experiences with the issues of trust, abuse, abandonment, control, love and judgment can all be created by addictions. Whether the addiction is to alcohol, drugs, food, sex or anything else, the resulting trauma and devastation can be the same.

I will share my favorite clipping. It has been on my refrigerator for so long that I forget who wrote it. Maybe it was Ann Landers or Dear Abby, but love and light to whoever wrote it, and thank you for your wisdom.

An Effective Solvent
Alcohol is a product of amazing versatility.
It will remove stains from designer clothes.
It will remove the clothes off your back.
If it is used in sufficient quantity, alcohol
will remove furniture from your home,
rugs from the floor, food from the table,

lining from your stomach, vision from the
eyes and judgment from the mind.
Alcohol will remove good reputations,
good jobs, good friends, happiness from
children's hearts, sanity, freedom, spouses,
relationships, man's ability to adjust and
live with his fellow man, and even life itself.
As a remover of things, alcohol has no equal.
(except maybe drugs)

Addictions have the ability to destroy any relationship.

We hear about the addictions of alcohol and drugs all of the time. Many of us have experienced the trauma and devastation that these addictions can bring to our lives. As victims of the addictive abuse, whether we are children or adults, the pain and feelings of helplessness are just as great.

The child is often confused and blames himself for the abuse and abandonment that he experiences. The child will then carry the damaged beliefs created by these actions throughout his life. These beliefs and patterns often create additional experiences with addictions in future relationships.

This choice is hard to understand, but in some way the soul agreed to endure the experiences with these addictions. This does not mean that you have no control of how these addictions affect your life. You are always in control of your choices and reactions as they can and will change the direction your life path will take.

It is possible that the person who came in to experience a life with the addict was the addict in a previous lifetime, and returned to this lifetime as the victim/survivor of the addiction.

This could give this person the opportunity to heal karma that was created between souls. I have also seen cases in which

Spirit explained to me that one soul loved another soul so much that they agreed to return, having advance knowledge of the challenge the addiction will present, to help this person heal a particular addiction.

I have met many souls such as these who work with Alcoholics Anonymous and other such groups healing themselves and assisting others in healing.

As a spouse or family member of an addict it is necessary to learn as much as you can about the problem and this can be done through the support and knowledge provided by Al Anon and other addiction appropriate support groups. This is your responsibility as part of loving yourself.

CHAPTER 8
PAST LIVES, CURRENT ISSUES

Realizing that the subject of past lives will challenge some of your belief systems, just as it did mine, I am going to share my clients' true stories of what they have experienced through past life regression; consider them as you establish your own beliefs.

Our past lives hold a magnitude of information, all of which can reflect on the lives we are currently living. We can carry karma, health issues, injuries or emotions from one life to another. If we fail to learn from the lessons that accompany the issues chosen for one lifetime, we carry them into the next one–or even the next ten; depending on how long it takes us to achieve healing.

This process often involves the same people from our soul group. Our previous lives may extend back thousands of years!

My knowledge of past lifetimes has been obtained through Spirit, as have all of my spiritual experiences. For me personally, the gifts of clairaudience and clairvoyance give me a different perspective.

When I ask to view a client's past life, I see a book open and the pages start flipping. Each page represents a lifetime. Sometimes the book is very thick and sometimes it is thin. This is determined by whether you are an old soul, having had many lifetimes or a young soul, having a lesser number. Each page is different, since there could be a few years, or even centuries, between lifetimes.

Not all of your lifetimes are relevant to this one, so as the pages are flipping by I tend to stop only on the lifetimes that are pertinent to current issues. Once the view stops on a page, it will appear like a movie or a photograph album. This is just one of the tools that Spirit has given me to help people gain a better understanding of their soul's existence. We have found it to be very beneficial in working with the issues of their life path.

Many people are able to use meditation to help access the treasure of information that our past lives hold. Your spirit guides and angels are eagerly awaiting you to ask for their assistance on your personal journey.

At this stage in your soul's journey, it is likely you have worked with all of the major issues throughout your many previous lifetimes, so the issues you are working on in this lifetime are not new to your soul's journey.

They may be carried forth from lifetimes hundreds or thousands of years back in your soul's history. It is not uncommon to get flashes of memory from past lives. These flashes can occur when you are experiencing a similar situation with the same person in this lifetime. If an injury or illness was a significant part of your previous lesson, it may be repeated in your present experience.

In striving to help people heal their emotional and physical ailments, I have discovered how important connecting with past lives can be. I may go into a soul memory to find where in the chain of lifetimes that particular injury or illness occurred. We could then work with that lifetime to discover what issues they were experiencing, as well as what beliefs were being created by them. This tool has proven to be invaluable in my work.

Through past life regression, we begin to understand and heal that lifetime, so that we can begin to clear the patterns of this life.

When working to heal your life path, you must first identify your issues; only then can you move forward to gain a deeper understanding of the issues, beliefs and patterns that you have chosen for this life. Many studies have been done of past life experiences and how they affect our current lives. Dr. Brian Weiss has written several books on this subject. When I first started working with Spirit, I really wasn't sure whether I accepted the idea of past lives. It just wasn't a part of my religious belief.

Abraham led me to Dr. Weiss' book *Many Lives, Many Masters,* which opened my eyes to a whole new world. Then I went to Abraham and asked for more information on this subject.

They taught me the importance of these past lives and how they affect our present ones, yet I was still skeptical. Spirit frequently uses the experience I have with clients to expand my knowledge and get me past my skepticism. In working with clients I would begin to see their past lives as if I were looking at a book about them.

Each page represented a lifetime, and I would just go into that lifetime observing, as a third party, what they had experienced. In sharing this knowledge with them, I was able to help them understand much more about why they were inexplicably attracted to some things and feared others.

Quite often in your current lifetime you will be drawn to the same experiences you have had before. This is Spirit's way of giving us a second chance; they will recreate the experience, giving us the opportunity to heal something we had been unable to heal in a previous lifetime.

If you feel compelled to be a soldier in this lifetime, it is likely that you have been a soldier in many past lifetimes, deriving a great feeling of accomplishment from the role. You may even feel drawn to a certain time period in which a war was fought, feeling a connection with that time in history.

There have been many occasions when I have had a vision of someone fighting in a battle of a particular war. I will see the uniform, the surrounding countryside, or sometimes the name of a country, and as I describe that war to the person, they excitedly admit to having an obsession with that particular time period. This indicated that they are still working with some of the issues created during that lifetime.

While working with one such client, in a vision, I saw him dying on the battlefield. He was going through his emotions of anger and guilt as he mourned the impending loss of his wife and children. He felt that he had abandoned his family in fear that he would be judged a coward for not fighting in the war. Spirit enabled me to see and feel all of his emotions, which helped me understand what issues he was working with in this lifetime.

Upon hearing my explanation, he could see the correlation between that lifetime and the lifetime that he was currently experiencing. He then explained to me the choices he made in this life. He worked at a job he hated, one that took him away from his family much of the time. The belief that he was not worthy of a family and fearing that he would fail them again caused him to stay disconnected from their love.

He was very focused on working hard so that others saw him as successful. Again, he was doing something to please others while abandoning his present family. This awareness brought such an understanding to him about what was really going on in his life that he was empowered to make a change. He was working with the issues of judgment and abandonment. By identifying his issues, he was given the knowledge to change his beliefs and the power to change his patterns for the better.

I have worked with several people and had their guides actually tell me that they did not want to come into this life as a certain gender. One such experience involved a female client. I could see where she had lived several lives as a man, and she had loved the power she felt in those lifetimes. As a man she had fought wars, ruled kingdoms, wielding power like a sword.

She then had to come into this life as a female (obviously to clear up the karma she created in those previous lifetimes), and she was totally rebelling, but to no avail. She put herself in a career field in constant competition with men. She had to find her power as a woman. This lesson was to prove to her self that women are of value, and that she could do something just as important through a woman's life as a man's.

She found, through meditation, that she could draw upon her knowledge and skills from the lessons of those previous lifetimes. She soon found that power was not about gender. It was about using wisdom and compassion to heal the challenges of life. That is being powerful!

My new ability to see and share information about past lives helped bring healing to my clients, but I wanted more. I felt that there must be a more effective way to do this work, so I asked Abraham for a way that I could help my clients experience their own past lifetimes.

By following Abraham's lead, I was taught a technique that I could use to enable my clients to walk through their own past lifetimes. When I guide them into their past life experiences, they are able to see who they were, as well as with whom they were interacting in that particular lifetime. While in this state of relaxation, they may see their surroundings, experience smells, or hear conversations that are going on in that lifetime. They can identify their gender and race as well as the time period of the life.

Quite frequently they are able to feel the emotions in the present that were being experienced at that time. I am usually able to see what they are seeing to help give them confirmation about their experience.

The purpose of this is that in identifying the issues that were blocking you in a past life, you are given an understanding of how that issue may be still blocking you in this life. The issue creates a belief; the belief forms blockages; the blockage then forms a pattern that may continue reoccurring throughout your life.

The knowledge gained from your past life enables you to release and heal the negative patterns in this life. These patterns are often keeping you entrenched in a place of dissatisfaction. If you are finding yourself or someone you love in this situation, it is necessary to release the blockages of this lifetime, thus changing the patterns you experience. I have found this method of healing to be quite helpful for many of my clients.

One of my first experiences with this method was with John. He had a very successful career until he entered a serious romantic relationship.

At that point, his work declined, as he no longer had his previous drive or interest in his work. This was a mystery to him, since he had previously been very successful. His concern brought him searching for answers.

When we asked his guides to take us back into a lifetime connected with this issue, we were both surprised at the clarity of the event. This past life occurred in the early 1800's, when he was forced to manage his family's general store in a small town, which he hated because he had bigger dreams. He had a wife and two little girls. He loved his wife and children, but he viewed the whole situation as a great responsibility that kept him from his dreams of freedom and great wealth. His dreams involved gambling, which was an addiction for him. We saw him in a saloon participating in a card game. We saw and felt his fear and frustration as he lost control and gambled away the family savings and eventually the family store.

Despair and guilt overwhelmed him, as he realized how he had failed in his responsibility to his family. He felt he could not face his family and friends, and we saw him walk, with rope in hand, to the outskirts of town, where he carried out his decision to hang himself. The amazing part was that both John and I could feel the emotions he was experiencing. Tears were running down both our cheeks.

To heal the issue and the beliefs that were created in that life, we had to identify the issue, which was responsibility. His addiction, gambling, prevented him from being responsible.

It actually represented freedom from his responsibilities. Responsibility produced the opportunity for failure. This failure brought many negative emotions and eventually his death in that lifetime. Amazingly, this paralleled his present lifetime, as prior to beginning his work with me, he had battled and conquered the addiction of alcohol.

During that difficult time, he repeatedly failed others by not taking responsibility for his life. His addiction was destroying this life. John eventually conquered his alcohol addiction and took control of his life.

John's life would ultimately hold many different types of addictions, as the addictions created opportunities to experience his issues of trust, abandonment, abuse, control, judgment, responsibility, and love. He had chosen all of the major ones. I often see this pattern in people who are the children of alcoholics or are alcoholics themselves.

When we use the word addiction, people frequently think of alcohol or drugs, but the addictions can come in many forms.

There are also addictions to sex, food, emotions or people. These are just a few of the additions we create in our lives. It may not be the specific person or situation you are addicted to, but the emotion that person or situation creates in you, that becomes your addiction.

John had experienced many relationships, but none like his current relationship. When this woman came into his life, he unexpectedly fell deeply in love. This love was unlike anything he had ever experienced. It held passion beyond his wildest dreams.

Through our regression, we discovered that this woman happened to be the same soul to whom he had been married in that previous lifetime when he abandoned her. This type of attraction often happens with connected soul mates; giving them **both** the opportunity to heal the karma that had been created between them previously.

In his love for her and his need to be with her, she became an addiction for him, in the same way as the gambling or the alcohol addiction. She became an excuse to avoid his responsibilities. He again found himself hiding behind his addictions. The power of his addictions created a fear in him that blocked him from taking control of his responsibilities. His addictions in the past had brought him fear, judgment, pain and loss of control, all leading up to self-worth issues that blocked his success and ended his life.

He may have loved this woman, but he had to heal this addiction so that he could release his blockage to responsibility and success. He was connected to this woman from his previous life. She was part of his soul group even to the extent of soul mate. On the soul level, she agreed to come back with him, to heal the karma between them as well as helping one another experience their issues, creating the opportunity to release and heal blockages in their respective lives.

Our soul is connected to our soul group throughout our soul's entire journey. This journey can span hundreds, sometimes thousands, of lifetimes. Our family members, spouses and friends are part of this soul group, as is anyone with whom we have a strong connection. Because this is all through divine agreement, you should appreciate them (even your exes) for the many learning experiences they have given you and will give you in the future.

Here is a story written by Jan about our past life regression work with her.

My experiences working with Linda have opened so many doors, not only for me but for my husband, two daughters and a son-in-law. There are so many stories I could tell, like the time Linda gave my son-in-law a message from a deceased relative that he never realized he had until he investigated it. That was spooky. She has given us confirmation that we have Spirit Guides and who they are. The experience that was life changing for me at least was when my husband and I did a past life regression with Linda.

Kenneth, my husband, and I had and do have issues with our parents. We had seen another person to help us heal our inner-child issues. In that work, I wrote a letter and intellectually forgave my mother and assumed that the negative energy with her had been corrected. However, I found that it was NOT. She still had the power to push my buttons and make me behave in negative ways that I regretted. I decided then to do an inner-child healing with Linda. It was so exceedingly powerful. I WAS that child again, lonely and emotionally neglected.

I could not control the tears and emotions, but this time I had someone THERE—Linda, seeing what I saw, feeling what I felt, and guiding me through it all in a very gentle way. I also learned in this session that I had issues with my Father, and to my great surprise, also my Father-in-law. I came away from that experience feeling emotionally healed, but I felt that something was still blocking me.

Linda then suggested that Kenneth and I do a Past Life Healing. I was very hesitant to do this, as I had at one time seen another person who recounted grisly past life experiences in which I had been tortured in a Nazi prison camp and of being an Irish immigrant of 13 whose mother (the same one I have now) choked her to death and threw her body into the ocean. Needless to say I did not want to experience anything that negative again!

The soul memories of those past lives had left me feeling angry and suspicious of my Mother's spirit. In reality, I was being hard-hearted and cold.

However, because of our past experiences, I trusted Linda implicitly and I wanted to heal or to discard any remaining deterrent and blockages from my childhood. This experience was totally different from my last past life experience. Instead of someone merely telling me of visions they had, I found that I was the one to have the visions.

Linda took me to a place of very deep relaxation. She began to tell me she would be seeing the same things and would guide me and help me if I became blocked. Before she finished telling me that, I saw a young girl, a child, with long dark hair and dark skin. I felt she was beloved by everyone in the palace. I knew I was in Egypt among the pyramids.

I told Linda what I was seeing and feeling, and that there was someone lurking who didn't like me. The next scene I saw was of this person standing over me with a knife. I remember the child's surprise and not understanding why this person hated me. I suddenly realized it was because they wanted their children to have what I had.

Linda asked me some other questions but before I could answer everything went blank. There was stillness; I couldn't see anything. Linda then explained I had died. She then took me back into the experience because she felt I needed to know who it was that killed me. I was afraid to go back, but she guided me to look deep into the person's eyes and to describe that person. When I described the grey blue eyes, I got the shock of my life. I had expected to see my Mother. What I saw were the eyes of my Father-in-law. This brought such understanding to the issues of our relationship!

Linda and I then went on. As she began to talk to me about going on to my next life, I was already there. I slipped easily into this Native American time. I was standing by the water feeling the presence of a predator. An older woman came before anything happened and we went back to camp. I found then that I had been sold or traded to an enemy warrior. I felt the emotion of my sadness since I loved the people of my village, but I knew I had no choice.

As I was watching this scene and I saw the warrior, I recognized him as being Raven of the Moon, my husband's spirit guide in this life. We were very much in love, unusually so for that culture. There were issues due to the fact that he was a powerful chieftain. I was young, foolish and unaware of all of the customs of that tribe. I became pregnant and gave him a son. His first wife and her brother plotted to be rid of me by making sure I transgressed the law.

I do not think I precisely saw how this was accomplished, but it involved a sacred buffalo robe. I was sentenced to death, but Raven of the Moon loved me so much that he killed me himself in a merciful way. As I looked at the situation, I strongly felt that my betrayers in that life were my Mother-in-law and Brother-in-law. Linda was trying to help me forgive Raven of the Moon realizing that he had killed me as an "act of love." Understanding the connection I have had with his spirit in this lifetime, I felt overwhelmed with love.

I wanted to quit then, but Linda guided me on, being told there was more to be healed. I knew then, as I went straight to it, that this must be that horrible Irish life I had been told about. I was again very young. I could actually feel a baby kick inside of me. I had been raped. We were very poor, my mother had many children and I was the oldest. I quickly recognized this woman as the same mother I have in this life.

But unlike what I had been told about this lifetime by someone else, I saw my mother grieving, worried over what to do. She was also worried about how people would treat me. This was very different from the bitterness and anger I had been told about. I saw my death as she tried to give me an abortion. Linda agreed, as she saw blood everywhere. That reinforced for me that through her guides, Linda was seeing everything I saw.

It was also comforting to know that while my mother's spirit in that life may have been incompetent and superficial, it was not that of a vengeful abuser. I saw, of course, the common threads of all of these lifetimes, death at a young age, the loss of children, the envy and jealousy of those around me, which has translated in a karmic way to this lifetime. In this life I have experienced betrayal by those driven by jealousy. But the main thing I came away with was an overwhelming feeling of love and healing of the spirit. I thank Linda for her assistance with this healing.

What Jan learned from her past life experiences was how she chose the issues of this lifetime and had been working with them through many lifetimes. Her issues of abandonment, trust, and judgment had controlled her life. She gained knowledge that enabled her to heal the emotional energy that had repeated itself over many lifetimes. This healing gave her the ability to change her future reactions to the experiences her issues will create.

While we were doing Jan's past life regression, her husband waited patiently in the next room anticipating his session. When we finished Jan's session, we didn't share any of it with Kenneth, not realizing what was to come. Here is Kenneth's story:

I had many sessions with Linda prior to this, but this is my experience with my past life session. Jan and I had visited with Linda a few weeks earlier, and Jan wanted to return and do a past life regression. Jan had her session first.

When it was my turn, nothing was discussed with me about what had occurred in her session. Linda surprised me by saying I needed to experience some past lives as part of my healing. I had read Dr. Weiss's books and knew of this method.

As Linda walked or talked me back into time, I wanted it to happen, but doubted that it would. As I lay there with eyes closed, Linda asked me about what I saw. I felt like I was possibly making it up, but I thought I saw myself riding a horse. I was an American Indian and was in the midst of a buffalo stampede riding as fast as I could with other Indians. If this was a hunt, I remembered no details. I began wondering if I was making this all up. Next I was around a campfire with my companions, including an impressive male figure whom I took as chief.

Linda asked me how old I was and I immediately knew I was four-teen and this was real. Though still not remembering details, I knew the hunt had been successful, and I had fulfilled a rite of passage. Linda asked me to look at the chief and see if I recognized him. I felt a father attachment to him or maybe he was the Raven. Linda asked me to look around and see if I recognized anyone. Amongst others milling around, I saw two women working on a buffalo hide. They reminded me of my mother and my aunt in my present life. They were obviously close to me in this life I was describing, but I knew I felt sadness for them.

I felt I had probably been raised by them and taught by them, but suddenly my stature was higher than theirs in this community because I was male and had been on a successful buffalo hunt. I felt some kind of loss and a lot of guilt.

As Linda moved me forward in the same life, I found myself with the rest of the tribe trudging along on foot in snow in an area with many small trees. In looking around I saw that the chief, Raven of the Moon, wasn't there and I realized I was now the leader, and we were in trouble.

We were tired and possibly starving. Linda asked if I recognized anyone. The two women from the previous scene were in front of me; they now had a lot of grey hair. One of them turned around to look at me. It was my Aunt Ruby from my present life. We were ever so slowly walking along, and then suddenly I felt (at that moment in my present life) my leg cramp and it was over. I had taken my last step and failed my tribe. I am feeling emotional as I write this.

Linda then brought me back in to the present and had me sit in a chair with a hematite stone to help ground me while she went to get Jan. I was sitting there starting to wonder again if I had made the whole thing up. Linda was very excited when relating to Jan what had happened. For the first time I realized Linda had actually been seeing what I had been relating. What Linda saw was that Jan and I had both been in the same life. Both Linda and Jan now told me the details of Jan's past life as an American Indian, killed after giving birth to a son. The Raven was her husband and my father. Jan had been my mother.

Somehow going through this past life regression had a healing effect on me, although intellectually I can't tell you how. I now understand why I find myself trying to take care of all the needs of everyone around me, as if I am trying to make up for failing my tribe.

I was particularly excited about these two past life regressions since they gave me great confirmation that past lives are real and how we continue to work with those of our soul group.

It helped Jan understand her issues and her connection with the people with whom she is still working. She had also received a better understanding of the purpose of her relationship with her husband. Jan and Kenneth agreed on a soul level to return in this lifetime to support each other in healing their issues, but, most importantly, it was to learn about their worthiness to receive love.

Raven of the Moon, Kenneth's spirit guide, who had been his father, had returned to assist them both in finding their spiritual path. It gave Kenneth a closer connection with his spirit guide, knowing that Raven of the Moon had actually been his father in a previous lifetime and made the choice to guide him through this lifetime.

Being the analytical one that Kenneth is, this is all very hard for him to process, but I have seen him growing on his spiritual path by leaps and bounds. He has only begun to discover the gifts he holds within himself.

Metaphysical Expos

Inasmuch as I met Jan and Kenneth at a Metaphysical Expo, I think this is a good place to tell about Expos. I had occasionally attended Metaphysical Expos with my daughter several years prior to discovering my gifts. I didn't understand any of it, as it all seemed so foreign to me and wasn't sure I even believed in this psychic stuff, but it was fun.

I always enjoyed people-watching and this was definitely the place for that. Once I began working with my spiritual gifts, the expos were where I made my connection with the many well-known intuitives who would eventually guide me on my spiritual path, as they became my role models and teachers.

I was soon to learn how very spiritual metaphysical expos/psychic fairs were. We had to laugh at my son-in-law when he described his impression of a psychic fair. He envisioned little tents being candle-lit, with a small table, a crystal ball and an old lady waiting to deceive you, the mystique of the television version. The persona of my motherly image definitely did not fit into that picture! I then understood why psychic fairs frighten people.

A metaphysical expo is a gathering of like-minded people sharing the gifts given to them by God. Yes, there can be fakes and "wannabes," but they will quickly fall away, as it is difficult to hold such negative energy in such a spiritual place and you have to enlist your intuitive instinct as to what is truth for you.

The energy at a fair can be overwhelming at first because the energy of Spirit truly envelopes the place. Spiritually gifted people fill the room, sharing their many different talents. Many of them are intuitively reading a deck of cards, telling you about your life and future; some do very detailed astrological readings based on your birthday and the planets. Some are even able to look at your palm and tell all kinds of information about your life. Others channel messages from Spirit, your angels and guides, or loved ones in spirit, as I do. There are often people at the fairs that do Reiki or some other type of energy healing work. It's rare, but a friend of mine does psychometry; she can take an item and intuitively tell you all about its history, as well as information about the person or people who owned it.

For me that is quite fascinating. Most of the larger Expos have books available to better inform you about all related subjects, as well as crystals, gems and many forms of intuitive talents. The gem and mineral vendors hold a wealth of information about the properties of their stones and are eager to share it.

When I first began my healing work, this type of event was the perfect place to share my gifts because people there were open to energy work and understood the benefits of Reiki. As my gifts developed more, I found myself sharing information that I was receiving from people's angels and guides as I was using the Reiki for the healing of their body.

Spirit then urged me to expand and do spiritual readings for people. Through these readings, I am able to give them messages from their angels and spirit guides. I would eventually gain the confidence to communicate with the other side, giving messages from loved ones in spirit. This all sounds pretty weird, doesn't it? Believe me, I thought so too!

Many times I don't understand the gifts that others have, just as I didn't understand my own.

I still don't understand everything that happens to me or around me, but I have learned to trust in God. At first I was not comfortable in what I felt to be a very unusual atmosphere, but I soon found the spirituality in it. I began to understand the importance of the messages we were giving to people and witnessed the tremendous healing we could bring to them, as all work was done through Spirit.

Many of you receive messages from your angels and guides daily, but don't understand how to connect with them. In my

Spirit readings, my messages may enlighten you to your life purpose, give you confirmation of a message you had been getting, or bring healing with a loved one in spirit. I love doing these events. I travel all over the country, and it is hard work, but it gives me the opportunity to touch the lives of thousands. Because my schedule has become so full, I have sadly had to cut back on the events I attend, but I am hoping that through these books I can enlighten many to a world beyond their present perception.

I have learned so much through the healing experiences of clients. I hear myself channeling the most amazing messages that are coming from their angels, guides, Spirit, and often loved ones who have crossed over.

One such instance happened that still leaves me amazed, because I had never heard of such an experience. My guides even told me to write it down for my future book. I was new on my spiritual path so I laughed at the thought of a book.

Laurie came to me very angry and with a major abandonment issue, which was understandable, as she had been physically abandoned by her family, and many of her friends through death.

She had experienced a series of failed relationships, often because she sabotaged them. She felt an inexplicable fear of trusting men, so she could not allow herself to have a healthy happy relationship for fear that they would abandon or betray her. This fear affected both her friendships as well as her career. Laurie had a difficult childhood that carried many scars of emotional damage from abandonment and abuse. She spoke of how she loved her father dearly and was devastated by his death.

When I suggested past life regression, she was skeptical, but willing.

After clearing and balancing her *chakras,* we began. She quickly moved into the lifetime her guides had chosen to show her. She was immediately shown her life as a woman. We were surprised to hear the woman called by the same first name, Laura. She began describing the experiences of this woman's life. She saw the woman's family, including four children and a husband.

Laura began, with great clarity, seeing many details of this woman's life. She was visually taken back into this woman's childhood while being given descriptions of family members. As usual, I was given the same vision, enabling me to guide her further through the experience.

She described her experiences with an abusive family. Laura was walking through this woman's life, having all of the thoughts and emotions flooding through her. Her experiences continued as she described the birth of her fifth child. We then witnessed her being brutally abused by her husband. This occurred soon after the birth of her fifth child, and she was not strong enough to recover.

As we watched her lie there, bleeding to death, she talked about her love for her children. She was very worried about the safety of her newborn baby. It was very traumatic for us to watch and feel what we both knew would soon be her death.

Laura and I were both exhausted, yet amazed, at what we had experienced. We were even more amazed when her guides explained to us that the woman named Laura in that past life, was actually her grandmother in this life. After the grandmother's death, she reincarnated back into the lives of her previous family, but living life as the granddaughter appropriately named after her.

Laura returned the next week very excited. She had done research with family members and gotten confirmation of the events and circumstances we had been told about. What Laura knew about her real grandmother was that she had died when her father was a baby. He had been raised by his father and step-mother.

When she reached out to her uncle for information about his early childhood, he told her stories she had never heard because her father had been too young to remember. The stories corre-lated with the similar events we had seen.

Her guides then explained to us that Laura's grandmother so wanted to complete her relationship with that family that she chose to return as her granddaughter. This also explained many of Laura's family issues. From the time she was a young child, the granddaughter Laura always had a compulsion to take care of her family.

Despite her painful childhood, she tried to maintain a close relationship with her father and uncles. Laura's issues of abuse, trust and abandonment from her previous lifetime were carried into this one, since she had been abused and emotionally aban-doned by her mother. Her father had physically abandoned the child to escape the constant battling with his wife.

Despite her father's treatment, she loved him and made excuses for his actions. But the emotional memories of the abused child kept her from trusting relationships. In Laura's healing process we implemented several different healing methods. We went back into Laura's previous life to gain understanding and heal the experiences of that lifetime, and then proceeded to heal-ing the present lifetime.

We assisted the inner-child in healing with both the spirit of her mother and her father. Laura's fear was a survival mecha-nism to protect herself. Laura's experience with past life regres-sion was only the first step on her path to healing, but most importantly, it gave her knowledge of what her purpose is in this lifetime.

We also uncovered in our work that in Laura's previous lifetime she had been tall, thin and strikingly beautiful. She believed that it was because of her appearance that her husband abused her while in his raging fits of jealousy.

In this lifetime Laura struggles with her excess weight. Her guides told us she had subconsciously created her body this way as a protection from the abuse of the past.

Laura's issues were trust, abuse and abandonment; through our work she was able to heal the pain of her emotional memories with her mother as well as the anger with her father for her childhood abandonment and his abandonment through death.

Children and Past lives

Children are often much more intuitive than adults. Unfortunately, not understanding this, adults make the mistake of not believing the stories they tell us of the past lives they remember.

Frequently, children have the ability to see angels, loved ones in spirit, and other beings. These things would frighten us, but to young children they seem normal, unless they are told otherwise. Their imaginary friends, as we call them, may actually be angels or guides that only they are able to see. Just as adults get flashes of memories from their past lives, so do children. But being so intuitive, their memories are often more vivid, allowing them to create stories to go along with them. Listen to your children, as the wisdom that comes from them is often channeled.

Rusty wrote to share this experience with her grandsons.

On a fall night in 1999, Rusty nestled in her bed to read a book by Sylvia Brown, a well-known psychic/author. The book talked about how younger children frequently and spontaneously begin recalling a former life.

The next day, Rusty was driving with her grandchildren, David and Scott, ages nine and seven, respectively. As they traveled, Scott, a precocious red head, suddenly exclaimed, "You know Grammy, when I was a brown haired boy, I went to a school that looked like that."

Stunned and more than a little curious, Rusty prodded him for further information. He said he couldn't recall details, except that his Mother was Mexican and his name was Max. Scott immediately lost interest in the conversation, so she turned to David, who does have brown hair, hoping to gain a greater insight. She said, "David, do you remember anything about this?" His reply was simply, "No, but I think he's right, his name was Max."

Six months later, Rusty's grandchildren were again visiting. The Health and Metaphysical Expo was being held, so she said, "Would you guys like to go see a lady who talks with angels?" Without hesitation, they were ready to go. When they got to the event, Linda Drake, who is generally booked every minute of the fair, miraculously had three immediate time slots available.

David wanted to go first and jumped in the chair. Linda gently took both of his hands in hers, closed her eyes and became silent. When she looked up, she looked at David, then at Scott, and back to David. She softly said, "This is so interesting. I have never seen this before. You boys have the same spirit guide. His name is Max."

To explain this particular situation more: The name Max was the name of one of the children when they shared a lifetime together. When I asked for more clarity I was told that Max was a grandfather the boy had been named after in that lifetime and both boys had a connection with the love of this spirit, and he was continuing to look after them.

This is another example of how Spirit touches the lives of children around us.

I received a call one day from a woman urgently needing a phone appointment. She said I had helped her tremendously a year earlier and couldn't think of anyone else who would understand her problem.

It was about her six-year-old daughter, Amanda. She said her daughter was very upset and was unable to sleep. The mother explained that she realized that her daughter was very gifted, but the little girl was complaining about seeing dark figures in her bedroom at night and was too scared to sleep.

The mother was at her wits'end, not knowing where to go to seek help. She was afraid if she took Amanda to a psychiatrist they would discourage any gifts her daughter had and cause her to shut down her intuitive spirit, as many gifted children do when challenged on the belief of their experiences by an authority figure.

I asked for a moment to connect with and to begin communicating with Amanda's spirit guides. I was confirming with them that there were no negative spirits or entities around the child that we should be worried about.

Then I heard a spirit voice also talking to me. The voice was that of a woman. She began to explain that what the child was seeing were the spirits of her deceased family members. This woman said that she was Amanda's grandmother. She explained that when alive she had been very spiritually gifted and had chosen to be Amanda's spiritual teacher. She said that Amanda was just beginning to see with her intuitive eye so things were still appearing dark to her.

Naturally we are afraid of images we see in the darkness. I asked her guides what we needed to do to help her not be afraid during her transition. They explained that it was time for her to begin working with her angels.

Poof, just like that, four angels appeared before me. Her guides told me that the angels needed to give the little girl their names so that she could feel more of a connection to them. Angels can take any form they want but these appeared to me as three small childlike ones and one grandmotherly looking one. They were delighted with the idea of naming themselves. (Angels do not have names as we are known by because they are energy beings created by God for each individual person.) I explained all of this to the mother and we waited for their decisions.

The first little angel decided she wanted to be called "Asja" and she spelled it for me, which I thought was a little strange but what the heck. When I told the mother this name with the spelling, she was quiet for a moment before she said that was the name they had considered for her daughter's middle name. The second little angel decided on the name "Daisy". When I shared this with the mother she gasped and exclaimed that Daisy was the name of their family pet that had recently died. The third little angel just couldn't make up her mind so I went on to the one with patient grandmotherly energy. She immediately chose the name of "Rose". The mother laughed and said the little girl loved picking roses from her garden. I turned back to the last little angel for her decision. She proudly said "Umbrella."

I said no, and explained that that wasn't a proper name for an angel. She insisted that Umbrella was what she wanted to be called. I explained this to the mother and she burst into laughter. She explained to me how her daughter had a love of umbrellas and carried one around all the time, especially to show off in pictures. The angel wanted to be named after something that the little girl loved.

Her spirit guides explained to me that the little girl needed to go shopping to find figurines to represent her angels. These were to be displayed around her bedroom so that she could connect with her angels and feel their protection.

The deceased grandmother requested that the mother bring out the family photograph album to show the little girl pictures of her grandmothers who had died before she was born and her uncle who had died as a child. These were the figures in the darkness that had come to visit her.

The mother was very pleased with our solution to her daughter's problem. It is helping the mother to understand that the grandmother was still with her, and even helping with the intuitive growth of her granddaughter. Many of us wish we had more of this type of help to assist us on our spiritual paths. I look forward to hearing more about this gifted little girl in the future.

Here is one more story of how children remember their past lives.

A woman came to me wishing to connect with her deceased father. Jenny's father had died when she was just five-years-old yet she had always felt a strong connection with him through dreams. We were able to receive many messages confirming that he was truly with us. Jenny came to work with me for other things but at each visit we would spend time connecting with her father.

After having a dream Jenny came to me to help her understand the meaning of it. In the dream, her mother and Jenny's two sons were with her as she visited her father, when he began to eagerly point to someone coming up behind them. She turned to see a young man approaching and waving to her.

He didn't look anything like her two sons, so she was curious as to who he was. Also in that dream, Jenny sensed that her father was eager to let her know that he would be moving on and that this would be the last time he would be seeing her in her dreams.

Jenny was naturally concerned that she may never see her father again, so she was anxious to interpret and verify the message from her father. Spirit did confirm that Jenny's father was trying to communicate to her that not only would she be having another son, but it would be her father's spirit returning into her life.

Jenny laughed at the idea as she already had two young sons with no plans for another. She was still sad to think that she may not see her father again. She had lost him physically as a child and now faced losing him again in her dreams.

A few months later, I received a call from Jenny anxiously wanting another appointment. Sure enough, she was pregnant just as her father predicted. He talked with us up until the last month of pregnancy. Jason arrived: a boy, just as her father had said.

A few years passed with little time to think about her father's prediction, when one day Jenny was reading a book to her little four-year-old son. Jason looked up at his mother with a big smile and said, "Mommy, I used to read this book to you when you were the little girl and I was your daddy."

Surprised by what her son had just said, Jenny needed more confirmation. She got out an old photograph album and began showing it to her son. As she flipped through the pages Jason quickly found a picture that Jenny hadn't seen in many years, explaining to Jenny that this was him as her daddy and that little girl was her. There was no way he could have ever seen a picture of his grandfather as Jenny's mother had remarried after his death and there were no original family photos displayed in there home.

If that weren't strange enough, the story goes on. A year later, as Jenny was driving with her three sons though an older part of the city that she lived in, Jason excitedly pointed out an old school building, telling Jenny that this is where he had gone to school when he was a little boy.

Her first thought was "that is impossible," but she called her mother anyway to check out the story. To Jenny's surprise, her mother verified Jason's statement. As a child her father had grown up in that neighborhood; in fact, he did attend that very school.

What a beautiful reunion Jenny has experienced though her relationship with her son.

Past lives

When working with people who wish to know more about their past lives, there are several ways in which you can make this connection. One of the ways is through a past life regression session. The method I use to help people visually walk through their past lives is accomplished through Spirit energy, but it can also be done with a hypnotherapist trained in past life regression work.

Another approach that some people enjoy is discovering their past lives for themselves.

This is done through accessing their *Akashic* records. This method is typically taught in Akashic Records classes. During this class, you are taught to connect with the Spirit Guides who oversee the Akashic Records. Akashic Records are our books of life.

They hold our soul's complete biological journey from day one and projected into our future. With the assistance of the Akashic Guides, and by following their rules, you are able to access the book of life for yourselves as well as others. I have taught this class for many years and always enjoy seeing the delight in people as their perception of the soul's journey is enlightened. You may even try reading books on the subject to see if you can learn to do this without the aid of a class. It is a lot of fun and a great way to begin working with your own intuitive gifts. We all have intuitive gifts to some extent. It is just a matter of being aware and learning to develop them.

CHAPTER 9
RESTORING THE JOY OF THE INNER CHILD

Journaling is one of the many methods of working with the inner-child. Writing about our memories and emotions is important, and prayer, as always, is beneficial during and after your healing period.

There are times when you must allow the child within you to come out and play. Go to a park and swing while talking with your inner- child. (If you choose to talk aloud, it is best to do it at a time when the park is empty!) The emotional damage that often envelopes our inner-child is seldom healed instantaneously. There is processing that goes along with the releasing.

Even when working with us, it may take the child several sessions to go through the healing process. After the releasing and initial healing have occurred, it is necessary for the adult to continue healing with the child. You must learn to respect and honor that part of you. **Your willingness to give your inner-child the love and nurturing that it deserves, is the first** step to loving yourself. Only when you love yourself will you feel worthy of receiving love from others.

There is a whole process that we go through in healing the inner-child, if you think there might be some abuse issues in your past, I do not suggest that it be done without a skilled counselor or a person trained in the process, since it uncovers and brings to the surface emotions that may need additional work in order to be healed.

This is a case shared by one of my clients about the healing of her inner-child. I have left the narrative in her own words:

I had no idea what to expect from my private session with Linda. We had talked in the past about doing "inner-child" work, so I was a little surprised when she started the session by asking me what was currently going on in my life.

I told her that what was bothering me were feelings of fear and insecurity regarding a friendship my partner had. We talked a little about it, and then she asked me to lie down on her massage table. I had my eyes closed, so I couldn't see what she was doing. She later told me it was energy work to get me to a deeply relaxed state. I was very relaxed, and she took me deeper and deeper into myself.

We talked about the feelings I was experiencing.

She asked if those feelings reminded me of another time in my life, and what words or images were coming to mind. I immediately began to recall a particular incident in my childhood. I became skeptical at this point. I was all too familiar with this incident and was certain I had done all of the necessary processing about it. In spite of this, in this relaxed state and with eyes closed, I kept going.

Linda enabled me to see myself at that time in my life. I was about five years old. My mother and I were at the house of some of my parents' neighbors. My mother was inside having coffee with the woman and I was playing in the garage. Linda guided me carefully through the remembering until I was fully in the experience. I was in the car being molested by our neighbor Mr. Jones. This was not a new memory for me, but it was either more information or a memory of another incident.

It was at this moment that the most amazing thing happened. In my re-experiencing of this on Linda's table, I was witnessing the event, I was there. Then suddenly, I saw my self outside the car, banging on the windshield, screaming and screaming into the car at me - the child being molested, trying to save myself.

I had never witnessed or experienced that splitting off before. It wasn't scary at all.

It touched me deeply to see myself trying to save me from this man. Linda continued to talk me through the experience until we processed completely out of it and back to the present. She helped me connect those "old" feelings and that experience, with my new fear and insecurity. I was then able to understand where my fear and trust issues had originated or had at least been experienced.

The most profound thing about this whole experience was that Linda "saw" the experience before I saw it, yet as soon as I began experiencing the emotions she was prepared to comfort me. Linda was touched just as deeply as I was, crying right along with me. Her seeing it first is what allowed her to guide me so tenderly through it. That session helped me to see the issues I was playing out at that time in my life because of that experience and the relationship I had with my family.

I've done a lot of work around these memories, but none compare to that day with Linda.

Since that first session, I have worked with Linda many more times. The next time we worked was again regarding the same man, Mr. Jones. Once Linda did the energy work on me and got me relaxed, we realized this session was for healing and forgiveness.

Linda invited Mr. Jones' higher-self/spirit into the space with us. In this safe space contained, created and held by Linda, I was able to *say to him what I needed to, allowing me to forgive, release and heal all of the horrible emotions I had harbored within me for so many years. She guided me in such a way that my fears just simply disappeared. I couldn't have done this work if Linda hadn't helped me feel so safe.*

Our next session was to work on issues with my mother. Our plan was to revisit the same experience we had been working on to see what my mother's role was, but Spirit had other plans. Again, in a trance-like state, I found myself in another childhood experience.

This time there were a lot of negative emotions directed at my mother. Linda tenderly and carefully guided me through the experience as well as gently coaxing when I was stuck. I saw and felt every detail of the situation. By feeling the child's emotions, I was able to express from my child's perspective what she needed to say to my mother. We achieved a tremendous amount of healing in that short session, when at the end of that session our higher-selves met and communicated what was needed in order to completely heal on a soul level.

I had received a spirit reading with Linda prior to this last session. I am always clear with Linda when she does my reading that I want to hear it all. When she looked at the cards she paused a moment and asked me how my mother was doing?

*I told Linda that my mother was having major health issues but just couldn't let go. Linda told me I really needed to finish my healing work with my mother to help my mother heal **her** part in our karma together.*

Linda explained to me that our karma of our relationship was what my mother's spirit was working on and that after we healed the karma, my mother would be free to cross over because it was her time to go "home". Two weeks after my healing session with Linda, my mother crossed over. As sad as it is to lose her, I am deeply honored and grateful to have done something that might have aided in her being set free from a body that no longer held any quality of life. I am so grateful to Linda for helping me through this healing but also to myself for having the courage to face something so painful. This healing has changed my life and how I relate in my relationships.

Do not let the part about her mother leaving scare you.

Just because you heal karma with someone does not mean they will die or leave your life, but it does enable you to have a better relationship with them. The releasing just means that the karma created between you has been healed, releasing the emotional blockages that were preventing you both from moving forward with your life path. In this case it freed her mother to continue on her soul's journey.

This is just one example of how the inner-child work can release the energy attached to our emotional memories. Through Spirit's guidance and healing energy, we were able to release the trauma of her childhood experience.

Iris's story of healing anger and abuse

Iris came to me asking for my help in healing with her father.

He was quite ill and was expected to die soon. She felt the importance of resolving her issues with him before he passed. Iris held so much anger with him from her childhood that she couldn't forgive him or herself. She knew this anger was blocking her life in many ways.

As we began unraveling Iris's life and its many turns, it was revealed that it wasn't her father with whom she was most angry. This is how it went: while growing up, Iris's mother had been depressed and angry and she drank a lot to deal with her unhappy situation. She took her frustration out on her family—nothing they did could please her. The mother's demeaning words of criticism were only the beginning of her abuse.

The children quickly learned to hide whenever possible to avoid her wrath, as did her husband. Iris's father was gone most of the time. He worked long hours, or so the family was told. At an early age, Iris took on the responsibility of taking care of her three siblings. She endured the battering abuse while trying to protect her younger siblings. Iris could not recall typical childhood experiences, as her memories were of responsibility, judgment and fear of failure.

Iris felt abandoned and betrayed by her father, who was seldom home to show them love or to protect them. The relationship between Iris's parents ended in divorce as her father retreated even further from their lives. Throughout Iris's life, she had made excuses for her mother's actions, yet was always quick to blame her father for the situation.

After her mother's death, Iris was overwhelmed with anger and grief that she could not explain. She pinned her anger on her father. Iris harbored a tremendous resentment toward her father because he had abandoned the family throughout their childhood.

After her mother's death, Iris's father tried to reconnect with his children, whom he barely knew. But Iris blocked his every move. He sadly retreated to what Iris saw as a fitting life without his family. Iris never received the love she was searching for from either her father or her mother. The abandonment from her father and the abuse from her mother reinforced her belief that she was unworthy of love and protection.

When we began working with Iris's inner-child, we encountered a tremendous amount of anger and guilt buried deep within the child. The child still had a great need to be loved, but her anger with both of her parents and her fear of being abandoned and betrayed was overwhelming.

In spite of the horrid treatment the mother had directed toward the children, she had been there for them. Despite the adult's grief over her mother's death, Iris needed to release the anger the inner-child continued to hold within her.

As for Iris's father, in the heart of the child, he had abandoned his family and the child continued to hold great anger over this. The child's anger was now creating her own abandonment to punish her father for what he had done.

We began the inner-child healing work, allowing the child to express and release the negative emotional memories she held with both parents. This enabled Iris to heal with her mother who was on the other side, as well as her father who longed to be a part of her life.

These are Iris's words:

My work with Linda was so beyond amazing there are no words to fully describe what she did. I know she is quick to give credit to God, but it is her gentle caring nature that encourages you to continue working through the tough parts.

Just knowing that she is there, holding your hand, understanding what you are going through, enables you to do healing you never thought possible. I had no idea why I was acting out in the ways that were making my life miserable. Through our sessions, I learned to understand the many different problems I had and how they were destroying my life and my happiness. She took me through the process of working with the inner child.

It was so powerful that the child I hold within me came out begging to heal, and could she talk!

I think I actually saw an image of my mother as she came to assist me in my healing with her, and in that healing I released emotions I didn't realize were hiding inside me. I was so shocked as I heard myself screaming and crying. I couldn't believe all of those emotions were in me, but I saw and felt the healing that came from that confrontation.

It was the healing with my father that made such changes in my life. I was able to see that it was my little girl's love for him and need for his love that was creating the anger. It was when we helped my little girl forgive her father that I was able to begin my process of forgiveness.

I finally began to understand who my father was and the abandonment he had experienced in losing his family. I found that I could truly forgive him and allow him to be a part of my life. The timing was an important factor, as my father died only four months after our reconciliation.

The following is a story about secrets hidden deep within the inner-child and the power of Reiki in healing the inner-child.

The use of Reiki (Universal Life Force Energy) to Heal Suppressed Memory Childhood Trauma:

Reiki healing energy can help heal the negative affects of suppressed childhood memories that haunt our subconscious mind. Many of us have experienced childhood trauma that cannot be remembered. The young mind, unable to cope with the trauma, suppresses the detailed memories of abuse. However, the affects of abuse are forever in our subconscious, affecting our actions and behaviors well throughout our adult lives. Reiki light energy has the ability to unlock the suppressed memory, providing the pathway to heal the suppressed trauma inflicted from abusive experiences.

Linda Drake has been very gifted with many healing talents.

For me one of her strongest gifts as a Reiki Master is the ability to channel the Universal Light Force Energy, in order to heal childhood trauma. My personal experience with Linda, is one in which I was healed from the negative feelings and thought patterns developed by being molested by a family friend at the age of four.

I had no recollection of the event until the age of 42, after one session with Linda. Having been plagued with depression, low self-esteem, and low self-worth throughout my life, I went to Linda to see if she could possibly help me. Gifted with the ability to see your past, and your "inner child" who holds all of our childhood experiences in our subconscious, Linda explained to me, "I see you as a little girl, and she is very, very angry. You have put her away on a shelf, not allowing her to live nor feel. Oh, and she has a secret…Who molested you Chris?"

Linda quickly put her hand over her mouth, as she was just as shocked by the question as I was. Linda said she wasn't sure where the question came from but that I should think it over.

This session definitely gave me something to think about.

I had few memories about my childhood, yet I did remember an adult male friend of my family's, who was especially friendly to me. He always gave me bright shiny quarters, pony rides on his lap and plenty of hugs and kisses. I recalled a conversation with my older sister in my 30's, in which my sister asked if I remembered how this man took both of us out on a walk back in the woods by his property. On the walk, he gave us piggy back rides, and he put his hands down the back of our pants and rubbed our bottoms. I did remember this incident, as well as him giving me a Cracker Jacks' plastic ring, and talking to me about our wedding night (I was 4, he was 40-50).

I had always down-played the incident in my mind, and just assumed that he was a major weirdo, that did not get the opportunity to do any harm. In the conversation with my sister, my sister did say to me, "Oh my God, you don't remember, Oh my God"…I swiftly ended the conversation, with my sister and chose not to talk to her about it again.

Now, with my first session with Linda, the memory of this man and his inappropriate attention to my sister and me was once again brought to the surface. Linda then told me to go home and at night to tell my inner child that she could trust me and show me what she needed to show me. Linda then performed a Reiki healing session on me. The Reiki was incredibly relaxing and I began to see beautiful colors, violet, purple and green. I felt a feeling of well-being and a sense of love that I had never felt before. I felt peace and protection.

The next day I left for a vacation with my two daughters. It was Thanksgiving weekend and I was on a trip to Disneyland. It was in the hotel room that night, after a wonderfully fun-packed day, that I told my inner child that she could trust me and that she could show me what she needed to show me.

As I began to drift off, the memories came flooding back like flashes from scenes in a movie. First, the incredible terror, footsteps of someone in our house and thinking that my parents are not at home; someone is in my parent's room, the floorboards are creaking. I cannot cry out, as there is no one to cry out to, my parents are gone, not at home. Something is being placed over my head like a nylon stocking...I am horrified and confused by someone in my bed with me....paralyzed with fear, I cannot move, nor understand the sensations of someone touching my privates, I am being molested. I am filled with guilt and shame.

The new knowledge of my traumatic past was liberating. The negative energy that it had taken to suppress my childhood secret had been immense. Unlocking the door to this deep dark chamber of my mind, was like lifting a million pounds off of my shoulders. I was now able to console this little child in my mind, and assure her that what had occurred was not her fault as she had always believed.

THE SECRET PATHWAY TO HEALING

With God All Thing Are Possible

My 16 year old daughter has a plaque on her wall which says what I firmly believe in. It reads "With God All Things Are Possible."

I continued to heal from my experience, seeing Linda for periodic Reiki Energy sessions and her process of healing my inner-child. I believe that God has provided us all, with this beautiful positive, energy healing ability, should we choose to develop it and use it, in order to correct the mistakes of the past. For those of us, such as me, who had an innate distrust of clinical methods of therapy, God provides us with an alternative method. If I had ever been willing to see a Psychiatrist, I believe it would have taken years to uncover what Linda's Reiki healing uncovered in one session. From this I believe that God can right a wrong with one sweep of His hand.

The Power of Reiki Universal Life Force Energy and Suppressed Memory

There have been many questions on suppressed memory, regarding court cases, and the power of suggestion by the therapist etc.

I would like to say that at no time did Linda ever describe a scene, or tell me what happened to me. She simply asked a question, and then told me to go and ask myself to find the answer. I must add, that in addition to my recollection of my molestation, I had additional memories and even clues that I had left for myself throughout the years that confirmed the truth.

It was as if I had left pieces of a puzzle all around, so that when the time came for me to accept this, I would have confirmation that it did occur. One such clue was a very distinct memory that I had of my Mother's wake and funeral when I was 14.

Devastated by my Mother's death, much of the funeral was a blur. However, I do intensely remember what happened the night of the wake after I went to bed. I awoke in total terror, shaking uncontrollably, as if I was shell-shocked. I could not ever remember what initiated such terror, and for years wondered what triggered it. After my trip to Disneyland, and my recollection, I began to think about this incident. Ironically, in my closet, after almost 28 years, was the logbook of the attendees to my Mother's wake (yeah, like everyone keeps that around for 28 years). I combed through the pages and found more confirmation: the signature of my perpetrator and his wife. It was probably the first time I had seen him in years, and just seeing him had traumatized me.

ENERGY HEALING-REIKI

It has been almost four years since my first session with Linda. My life has improved dramatically as the anger I felt from the past is gone. I am now able to attract positive relationships into my life and look forward to my future.

Having had this experience has always left me feeling honored. Yes honored, because I am one of the lucky ones. I did not commit suicide, but instead was shown the method to heal the deep, wounds that I carried, and stop the cycle. I have taken Reiki I & II and it is my hope, that as I develop my skills that I too, be able to help others that may have experienced what I have.

Christina's story was an amazing one as she was given the opportunity to heal the many issues she had chosen for this lifetime. In working with the inner-child we were able to access blocked memories creating a healing that was not otherwise possible. Christina was able to establish a relationship and a love for this aspect of her self.

As we worked through her childhood experiences, we saw that she had chosen all of the major issues for this lifetime. We worked through her relationships one by one as she was able to release her anger and the belief that she was unworthy of love. Christina found that she was able to overcome the negative relationships of her past, releasing the beliefs and breaking the detrimental patterns she had developed. Through this work Christina also learned to love and appreciate who she was as a person and a mother. Christina now has an awareness of the challenges she chose for this lifetime and the power to control her destiny as she now creates the life that she desires.

This is a great time to begin your inner-child journal of healing. You will eventually have several different journals.

This is the worksheet that I ask my clients to begin their healing work with.

INNER-CHILD WORK SHEET

Find a picture of yourself as a child (about 5-7 yrs of age or a significant age) make a 2"x3" copy of the picture with the face of the child showing.

Put this picture in the center of a sheet of paper. On the left side of the picture write, **Positive About the Adult,** on this side write all of the positive things or words that you can think of describing you as a child. On the right side of the picture write, **Positive About the Adult,** on this side write all of the positive things you can think of about the adult. Below each word note whom you associate this description with.

One the next page draw a line down the center, to the left side of the line write **Negative About the Child,** noting all of the negative words, emotions or thoughts associated with your child memories. On the right side of the page, write **Negative About the Adult,** noting all of the positive words, emotions or thoughts associated with your child memories. Take your time in doing this and make notes beside the words as to whom you associate these words or actions with.

This is the time to begin connecting with your inner-child. The inner-child truly is an aspect of you, having an energy and consciousness just as you currently do. The inner-child is connected to the physically and emotionally energy of all that it experienced. This child is an important part of you, as well as the key to your healing any negativity that you experienced from your childhood up to today.

It is helpful to make multiple pictures of the child to post around the house as a reminder of the work you are doing and to better connect with the inner-child. Some people have a difficult time talking to a picture of themselves, as a child. You may prefer to work with a stuffed animal or baby doll as something you can hold or better visualize while you are talking to the child.

Give the child life by visualizing and reminiscing about happy memories. Talk to the child in a loving nurturing way. This child needs you just as much as you need the connection with the child within you. If you really want to do healing with your inner-child, make a commitment with the child to spend time talking to the child multiple days a week (as many as possible is most helpful). As you increase the time spent with the inner-child you will become more comfortable with his or her emotions. This is also teaching **you** how to love yourself by learning to identify your needs and taking the next step to meet those needs.

Do not be surprised if you begin receiving messages from your inner-child, this is our goal. These may come through thoughts, memories, emotions or even cravings. As one of my clients began working with her inner-child, she found herself having unusual cravings for ice cream. This occurred after each of our sessions, as if the child wanted to be rewarded for helping us do the healing work. The adult would feel this child-like happiness, and joy come over her following our sessions and there was that craving for ice cream.

CHAPTER 10
SOUL GROUPS AND SOUL MATES

As Spirit explains to me, there is a finite or fixed number of souls, and **each** of these souls is a part of the God consciousness. Each soul will experience an infinite number of lives, determined by the path of growth it pursues and karma it heals in each lifetime. This progression of lifetimes continues until they have achieved a position of unconditional love or completed all of their karma.

SOUL GROUPS

Throughout this book I talk about *soul groups*. Our soul group is one of our support groups. It includes the souls with whom you have a connection. Your soul travels through many lifetimes with this group, which may be made up of hundreds or thousands of souls.

There are rings of souls within our soul group. The inner rings include the souls with whom you will have the closest connection throughout your lifetime. Often, on meeting one of these souls for the first time, you may feel an immediate connection. There is recognition on a soul level. You may have an unexplainable way of sensing the others' needs. (Do you ever call someone and they say they were just thinking about you?)

The soul group rings of familiarity spiral out from your closest friends and family to marriage partners to brief acquaintances that you may only interact with one time. But even that one time could have a major effect in your life or theirs.

Each of you is working on certain issues and these other souls are helping you with yours, as you are doing the same for them. There is unfinished karma between you, and your interaction allows for a healing of this karma. The roles you play throughout your soul's journey through its many lifetimes are interchangeable. In referring to the relationship between two souls, your role in one life may be to play the mother, while in the next life you are the daughter.

This explains why we occasionally see a mother/child relationship where the child just naturally seems to have more of the mothering traits. Both parties are continuing the issues of a previous life through their experiences of this lifetime, but for some reason they needed to trade places. Your gender may change to meet the needs of that lifetime.

The soul connections are not limited to family. They may be friends, teachers, fellow workers, or neighbors. They can be anyone around you with whom you interact.

These interactions provide the experiences that are necessary to work on your issues.

We generally stay within our soul groups to experience our major issues, but occasionally I work with someone who has chosen to interact with a different soul group. There is a purpose for this choice. For some reason, the issue or issues they have chosen to work with in this lifetime cannot be experienced within their own soul group. This is easily recognized when a person feels that he does not connect with his family. He may feel a lack of emotional closeness to them, or even see a dramatic difference between his actions and the way they act or think.

Nonetheless, he chose that family for what he needed to learn from the experience, or what they were to learn from him. This does not mean that he will stay disconnected from his soul group for his entire life. He will eventually be reunited, to feel the comfort and support of his original soul group.

When you connect with someone of your own soul group, it can be like finding your best friend. This happened for Judy at a point in her life when she was dealing with a lot of her issues. She was coming out of a marriage that involved control, emotional abuse and abandonment. She felt that everyone judged negatively her for her difficult decisions, causing her to have very little faith in herself.

In Judy's search for a place to live, Spirit led her to Pam, who had a room for rent.

They recognized the soul connection between them immediately and quickly became best friends. Pam was there to give Judy the friendship and emotional support she desperately needed while Judy rebuilt her confidence and her life. As their friendship grew, Judy soon found her purpose in their relationship as she was there to help Pam through a struggle with her career and a troubled relationship.

This was not a coincidence. It is just one way we are reunited with those in our soul group, helping each other work through the challenges of our issues. Judy and Pam's friendship has continued through the years, as they each continue to support the other one with the challenges of their lives.

An interesting soul group story happened to Beth when we did a past life regression. When Beth first came to me, she was depressed, having just gone through a very messy, painful divorce.

She wanted to heal the residual negative emotions from the relationship and cut the energetic cords that existed between them. Beth had heard about my work and came to the appointment quite curious about what I could do for her. She admittedly went into the session feeling skeptical and doubting it would work for her. She wanted to see what the karma was between her and her ex-husband from previous lifetimes so we decided to try past life regression.

She later described her surprise, and she said it was like watching a movie. She quickly found herself in a previous life where she was a young woman with two small children. She was married to a man who was very controlling and had a quick temper. She sensed that he loved her and the children, but he didn't know how to show it.

As her life flashed by, she went from scene to scene, describing what she saw and felt. Her husband was in a business partnership with his best friend. However, there was a fight between them in which her husband was accidentally killed.

After her husband's death, the business partner proceeded to cheat her out of everything. She lost her husband's share of the business, their money, their home, and all of her possessions.

She soon found herself destitute and on the streets struggling to take care of her two children. Beth was overwhelmed with sadness as she saw this woman's desperate struggle with life. In that lifetime, she acknowledged that she experienced issues of trust, abandonment and control. In her regression to that past life, she recognized her past-life husband to be her present-day father, and the business partner to be her present ex-husband.

All of the pieces started falling into place as she came to an understanding of how karma was playing out between the lives.

Spirit showed her the correlation between the lives. In this life she had been married to James, a very driven man who showed his love in a controlling way. He loved his family, but in striving to show his love by meeting all of their basic needs, he became a workaholic.

His family did not understand this effort as being love because they were searching for emotional love. Although the money he earned provided Beth and their children with the security and possessions he had taken away in the previous lifetime, his choosing to work all of the time made them feel abandoned, betrayed and unloved.

Neither Beth nor James understood the other's definition of love. The marriage ended in divorce, and they both lost their most precious possessions. She lost the marriage, love and security that were so important to her in this lifetime, and he lost his family and part of the business they had worked so hard to build. In this lifetime, he had karma to repay for all that he had taken from her in the previous lifetime.

SOUL MATES

Now we come to soul mates, a popular buzz word at this time.

On the spiritual level, I am told that your soul mate is a soul with whom you have a special connection, more than just the typical connection to someone in your soul group. A soul mate appears in your life to assist you in healing the karma you each created in a previous lifetime or in many previous lifetimes.

A soul mate is a soul who is committed to helping you work on the challenges of your issues. Because of our many issues, we may choose many soul mates to interact with in one lifetime. They have a purpose in your life, as you do in theirs.

The special connection between soul mates is often found in intimate relationships, but is not limited to them. Sometimes a soul mate can be our best friend and the relationship can extend through many lifetimes. Occasionally you are lucky enough to have a soul mate that is both your partner and best friend. Soul mates are together by agreement. They can be there for you as you experience your issues, or they may be there to help create experiences from which you learn and heal. Both roles are equally important. You will play this same type of role in their life.

The connection between soul mates can be sudden and overwhelming. Sometimes, before we are aware of what is happening—bam! They are in your life.

The energy can be so highly charged between two soul mates that they forget to utilize their common sense. You may feel the connection as soon as you lay eyes on one another or even hear their voice. That emotion is represented by the term "love at first sight." The attraction is unexplainable because it is on a soul level. Watch out, because although the emotional and physical attraction may be great, they are not always meant to be a permanent part of our lives!

Often they come into our lives when we are stuck, to wake us up. Sometimes they remind us of who we really are, or what we really need.

Your higher-self is drawing them to you for some reason. For instance, that issue you had been avoiding—well, here is your lesson, time to wake up and become more aware of what is going on in your life. Sometimes, it is to help us heal, or to move us forward in our lives by bringing an experience to us to make us address issues that are holding us back. They will even bring challenges to us that will enable us to get out of a difficult situation that we are refusing to acknowledge.

The attraction between soul mates is not always immediate, but the emotions will always be strong. You may feel an immediate dislike or irritation and try your best to avoid that person, but life will continue to throw you together. Often this is because you are mirrors for each other; the traits you dislike most in him are often your issues, the very issues that you came into this life to heal.

The following examples demonstrate how powerful and often difficult relationships with our soul mates can be.

People often think of their soul mate as someone just like themselves and believe that life with their soul mate should always be smooth sailing; but the truth can be quite the opposite. Our soul mates and those from our soul group can really push our buttons, as that is their purpose in our life. We are not going to learn from relationships that rarely challenge us.

Karen and Julie's soul mate experience

The following describes such a relationship between soul mates: Karen met Julie at a retreat where they were both pursuing advancement along their spiritual path. They felt an immediate connection, and quickly became best friends. I had multiple sessions with Karen before she brought Julie to see me.

When Karen introduced Julie to me, I was stunned. I immediately began to see a lifetime that they had experienced together begin playing out before me, in what I call a vision. It always fascinates me how past lives work.

I began sharing with them the connection that I was seeing between them, and what that lifetime had held. As the scenes were played out, I saw two little girls; Julie was the oldest, about eight, and Karen, about six. Julie had matted blonde hair and Karen light brown curls. They were sitting in a yard, happily playing. But their frail, thin, dirty bodies clothed in ragged dresses told another story.

As their story began playing out like a movie, I saw the many types of abuse they, as sisters in that lifetime, had endured at their mother's hand. She had emotional problems that made life a living hell for her, and she often vented those feelings on her two little girls.

After enduring several years of this trauma, the girls were eventually taken away from the mother, who was placed in a mental hospital. Despite her abuse, they loved their mother and were devastated by what they felt as her abandonment. After being removed from their mother, the circumstances of their lives changed for the better, but they carried the beliefs and patterns created by their mother's abuse of them and subsequent abandonment. The issues they had chosen to work with in this lifetime were abuse, abandonment, trust, control, judgment, and love.

Experiences with these issues would continue as opportunities to learn about and heal the karma of the issues. This knowledge empowers the person to change the patterns of the past thus changing the experiences of the future.

At the time I shared this story with them, I had no idea that in their present lifetimes they had each experienced very traumatic childhoods, similar to their past lifetime together. They each had experienced major issues with abusive mothers. Their present childhoods had included the same issues of trust, abuse, abandonment, control and judgment, all further creating negative worthiness beliefs which prevented them from being able to fully give and receive love. It became obvious that they were both still working on the issues of their previous lifetimes. We were all stunned by this revelation.

Everything started to make so much sense to all of us. I began to work with them individually. We proceeded through the process of healing the negative emotional memories from their current and past lifetimes.

Our negative emotional memories are formed in layers, like an onion. Even as we think we have finished our healing process with emotional memories of our past, our life path continues to hold the same issues we chose in the beginning. The healing we achieve is demonstrated through our actions. How we react to our experiences with those issues is our choice and we will be continually tested by our higher-selves to see if we need more healing with that issue. Until we fully heal an issue and it no longer holds control over us, our spirits/higher-selves continue to draw experiences to us, through which we are challenged again and again to heal that issue.

This is exactly what happened for Karen and Julie, even though they both did healing with their respective mothers.

Their issues of trust, abandonment, abuse and control were still a part of their life plan. Being reunited in this lifetime was not coincidental. They were actually soul mates that came together as best friends. Considering this close connection, they allowed themselves to trust one another.

A major factor in a soul mate relationship is each allowing themselves to trust and be vulnerable, letting down all armor of defense. Trust was a major issue for both Karen and Julie, considering the history of their childhood abuse.

Their relationship became a testing ground for their higher-selves to gauge how they were doing with the healing of their issues. Conflicts would arise, with each unconsciously retreating to the old emotional memories of abuse and abandonment. Their trust for each other created a situation between them as they soon found themselves in a situation of being used and abused by each other, much like the abuse they experienced as children. For a brief time, they would forget the trust of their soul mate relationship.

What their experience demonstrated to them was that they still had work to do on their issues to better understand how their issues can control and often create havoc in our lives.

This may seem abusive in itself, but it is the purpose of a soul mate relationship. It is someone who we trust enough to allow ourselves to be vulnerable. With our shield of protection in front of us, what do we learn? Only through the soul agreement of this strong connection will we be able to endure the experiences of our issues in addition to giving ourselves the opportunity to learn from them.

Our relationships enable us to heal or bring completion to unfinished karma.

I hate it when I read an unfamiliar word or term, and I have to stop the flow of my reading to look it up, so I will save you the trouble on "higher-self." Throughout this book, Spirit will use the term "higher-self." Here is our definition:

The term "higher-self" is only one of many names for the highest level of the human existence. The higher-self is the soul within us that remembers the life plan that we created and creates the energy to motivate us into the experiences of our issues. Modern science is beginning to understand the ancient teachings that energy flows from the higher-self into the body's seven energy centers known as *chakras*. This energy field affects the entire body—emotional, physical and mental. It will direct energy and awareness into our human consciousness at the appropriate time, drawing to us the opportunity to experience the issues of our chosen path.

When we are in alignment with our higher-selves, we are living in harmony with our life purpose. We live with the maximum love and life force energy that our higher-self desires.

I am often asked, how do we communicate with our higher-self? I went to Spirit for a good answer on this one. Your higher-self is the part of your existence that is one with God. It is your spiritual self that yearns to achieve all that you can as you walk on your path of life. It motivates your thoughts and emotions. To whom do you reach in your time of need? For most of us, it is God, in some form.

As you pray to God, you are also speaking to your higher-self. God gives the higher-self, or soul within us, the strength and power to create, endure, and conquer our biggest challenges.

God never abandons us, as our soul will not abandon our human body until the time of our passing. Clarity of thought is brought forth from a quiet state such as from meditation as it is the best form of communication with our higher-self. Our higher-self is a part of our mind, so we communicate with it on a constant level. Sometimes we find ourselves feeling disconnected from our higher-self as we struggle in our lives of chaos, finding ourselves or parts of our lives out of control.

When we create conflict between our higher-self and our human body, we often experience physical illness, and manifestations such as disease or pain. This is our soul's way of getting our attention. Your spirit guides work in conjunction with your higher-self to guide you through your daily life. The best way to stay in harmony is to listen and follow their direction.

The following is another example of soul mates being reunited:

Joan had gone through a very difficult marriage in which she experienced abuse, judgment and abandonment as her primary issues.

Although she finally ended the marriage, after 22 years of accepting this treatment, her self-worth was depleted. Joan was struggling in her search for happiness and fulfillment. She couldn't imagine anyone giving her a second look, much less a tall good- looking, rugged cowboy.

But from the moment Joan set eyes on him, there was an undeniable attraction between them. Cowboy Jim did all the right things–not only did he lavish her with flowers and gifts, he also gave her the positive attention she hadn't had in years. He aroused emotions in Joan that she thought were long forgotten. She remembered what it felt like to be a desirable woman again, and did it feel great! The passion between them, when together, spread through both of them like a wildfire.

Jim's actions reminded her that she was important and that she deserved to have her needs met in a relationship.

Through her relationship with Jim, Joan's feelings of confidence and self-worth were repaired and she remembered how to love herself again. They had a great time together but soon figured out that the passion they both felt was their renewed passion for life.

There was a purpose for their encounter in this life. On a soul level, Jim had enabled her to receive this great gift of healing, even though the timing wasn't right for them to be back together in a permanent relationship. This often happens when two souls have been together in one or more past lives. They come back together, reuniting with the same passion they had previously experienced. Sometimes the connection is an opportunity to finish a lesson they were working on in a previous life, or maybe just to bring healing to issues for one or both of them in this life.

Either way, Joan will tell you, a good cowboy comes in handy every once in a while!

A soul mate often appears in our life during the darkest of times.

This was true for Eric. When he came to me, he felt he was in a dilemma, not knowing what to do about the mess he felt his life was in. He had been laid off from his job for about six months, searching to no avail for another. His self-worth was diminished by the fact that he felt he was failing to support his family.

Eric had suffered a traumatic childhood of abuse and abandonment. He had always had a difficult time with relationships because he learned at a young age not to trust love. Because of his abandonment issues, his loss of family and friends created an even bigger fear of closeness. Eric's fear of vulnerability created a shield.

He hid behind the protective shield, not allowing anyone to get close enough to love him. His fear was so great that he would use a tough image as his shield. He would often sabotage his relationships if he felt he was in danger of getting hurt. It was actually his wounded child that was controlling him.

His fear was so huge that he found himself repeatedly sacrificing his opportunities for love and happiness. Eric found his soul mate, complete with that magnetic attraction that soul mates can have.

But his fears often sabotaged the relationship, as they worked through many challenges. Having been abused and abandoned as a child, deep down he held the belief that he was not worthy of love. Eric was given the family, with its love and acceptance, that he had always desired, but he still feared he was not worthy of their love. He was gifted with three children to teach him about unconditional love, as small children do. In his time of challenge, he began doubting himself.

At a time when he was at his lowest point, another soul mate entered his life. Neither of them realized the purpose of the relationship. He was drawn to her at first as a friend. They were both experiencing a difficult time of their lives.

There was no pressure or responsibility to their relationship, which felt perfect for Eric because there was no opportunity for failure. Their relationship involved fun and laughter making it an escape from reality. They came into one another's lives to boost each other's ego and help each other heal from a painful and challenging situation.

As Eric had a pattern of doing, he began sabotaging his marriage. Not believing himself to be worthy of unconditional love and support, he tried to push his wife and children away because of his fear of failure.

He began recreating the patterns of abandonment from his childhood. These are the lessons of his issues. The relationship with his reunited soul mate became an illusion that met their needs at the time. Unfortunately the attraction and emotions of a soul mate relationship are created to meet our needs at that time. Good or bad, there is a burst of energy for our lives that a soul mate can bring to us. They often come into our lives to remind us of our true value and the importance of our dreams.

We just have to be careful that we don't get carried away allowing the illusion it may create to distract us from our true path. Eric had chosen to experience the issues of trust, abandonment, abuse, responsibility, and love, so this was exactly what he had been experiencing in relationships throughout his life.

This is where we must understand the value of our soul mates. The first soul mate came into Eric's life to work together on their issues. Then the second came in to heal the injured soul so that he could continue working with the issues of his path. At this point he must make a choice.

Whichever soul mate Eric chooses, the patterns will continue until he heals the emotional memories and beliefs that were created in his childhood.

These are the blockages of his life. By working with his inner-child, we gave the child the tools to heal his patterns. Eric's second soul mate presented him with the opportunity to learn about and heal his issues. He has the choice of **reacting** from childhood emotional memories as he had in his previous life choices, or making conscious decisions using the knowledge and healing he has gained, to **act** in a way that is best for his life.

For Cindy, this is how her life's path brought her at least two soul mates, as well as many from her soul group, to help her.

Cindy had chosen to experience many issues in this lifetime. Number one on her list was control; this is a hard one, as it is connected to many of the others. The first of her soul group to experience this with her was her father.

There were many things about her father that she admired, but he had his own issue of control, so they experienced their issues together. Cindy came into this life stubborn, hardheaded, and strong willed. These were all tools needed for her lessons of control. Her father didn't know what to do with a strong-willed daughter. Breaking her will by way of control seemed to be the easiest solution for him. It was a challenge for both as she fought and battled her way through childhood.

If she had been complacent, there would have been no experiences with control for her to teach her.

As a result of her experience with her father, Cindy soon came to the belief that love was shown through control, intimidation, and judgment. In her search for her soul mate she found the perfect one, a relationship through which she would experience her issues. With a soul mate, you are often drawn to each other like magnets.

Cindy was so blinded by love at first sight (Spirit's trick to get people together) that she didn't notice that her new love had the same traits as her father; both the traits she admired and the ones that challenged her. She spent many years working through the experiences created by her issues.

Spirit continued to put people from her soul group in her path to help her learn from and heal her issue of control, as well as other significant issues.

Cindy's experiences taught her to work from both sides of the issue. As the plan unfolded, Cindy had also chosen to experience life with a strong-willed daughter with the same issues as Cindy and her father. Talk about challenges, they came from all directions.

During the many years of experiencing these issues, Cindy's self-esteem and self-worth were destroyed. Her perception that love involved control, judgment, and abandonment had destroyed her self-worth, her marriage, and her family. To survive, she had to somehow empower herself. This meant finding respect and love for herself. Never having done this before she wasn't sure where to start. Cindy's history with relationships had taught her that she could not trust others to meet her needs. So Cindy began controlling her life by pushing everyone away, but in doing so, she denied herself of love and acceptance, making her lonely and unhappy so she was confused.

Now that Cindy was in full control of her life, she panicked at the prospect of her future. She had never been in full control before. Her insecurity and fears kept whispering to her, "What if you fail?"

The lessons that accompany our issues can be painful.

But as humans we learn to pay attention when something creates enough pain. Spirit has their way of getting our attention, and sometimes it takes being hit by that spiritual 2X4 to teach us our lesson. God is a merciful god. Our lessons with life start out small, becoming larger as we fail to listen. If we do not pay attention to the small one, we are then given the spiritual 2X4, (THE REALLY BIG LESSONS) which we can't ignore.

Cindy had to deal with fear and uncertainty, but at least she was in control of where her life was going. This was a lesson in confidence for her.

As always, Spirit had a plan. They brought another soul mate into her life. She had known this man before, but only as a friend. But this time there was that undeniable attraction for both of them. This soul mate came into her life at this particular time for a special purpose: Cindy had learned her life lesson through her experiences with control in her first marriage.

She was now ready to heal and move forward with her next life lessons. This person was placed in her life to give her the love and support necessary for what her life was to hold. This is not saying that her issue of control was gone, but she now makes different choices in how she reacts to experiences involving control.

You are probably wondering why she didn't fall in love with the second man in the first place if he was also her soul mate. The timing was not right. She first needed to learn from the experiences that the first soul mate brought, healing the karma of her issues. She could have carried the experiences and patterns of control through many different soul mate relationships (which some of us do), but she chose to work through her issues with just two soul mates.

Cindy has moved forward, continuing to experience lessons with her issues. But because of her healing work, she has the knowledge to make better choices involving her issues. She now has a relationship with a soul mate that enables her to be in her power, supporting her with love and acceptance.

Cindy's story was a perfect example of soul groups and soul mates. There are no mistakes, you did not come into your family by coincidence, nor did you marry that husband or wife by mistake.

There is a purpose for every relationship. Relationships give you the opportunity to work on your issues as they can bring you challenges and healing. Don't misunderstand; the lessons of your issues do not always have to be painful. Sometimes part of your life purpose is to teach others to receive love. This lesson may come through a relationship with a mate or your own child.

I will share with you a heart-touching story. Ellen had a very difficult childhood. Her family life held abuse, abandonment, fear, and control. The experience of unconditional love was not a part of her life. Because of this, she really did not know how to give love or to receive it. Ellen desired to have love in her life, but she could not trust or accept the love that was given to her. Nor did she know how to show love to others.

She married a very patient man who loved her very much. Because of her childhood experience, when she became pregnant, she began having a difficult time with the idea of parenthood.

Ellen's greatest fear was of being like her parents. She felt she had nothing to give a child. God knew better and gave her the greatest gift. James came into her life as a special child: being a Down's Syndrome child, he just overflowed with love and laughter. James was her soul mate. The connection between them was unmistakable. He chose to come into her life as her lesson about love. Seeing how James loved her and everyone else unconditionally changed how Ellen saw love. There was no judgment in the child's love, so this helped Ellen heal her belief that she was not worthy of love.

Ellen originally came to me to help her with her fears of parenthood. Through the work we did with Ellen's inner-child and the unconditional love she received from James, she learned to forgive people for their faults, helping her release her anger and trust issues. She then began receiving love, and trusted that when she opened up to love others, she would not be abandoned.

The changes this made to Ellen's relationship with her husband were phenomenal. James' spirit chose to teach others to receive love through his challenges as part of his life plan. The lesson of love that he gave to others was invaluable. He brought a special healing to every life he touched. We thank God that he gives us special people such as James.

CHAPTER 11
THE PROCESS OF HEALING AND THE TOOLS

REIKI

I highly recommend you prepare for your healing process by utilizing the gifts of a Reiki practitioner or a similar energy healing technique. The clearing and releasing of blocked energy in your *chakras* promotes the processing of emotions, helping you quickly move along your healing path. In searching your area for a Reiki practitioner, you may note that many massage therapists now incorporate Reiki into their work.

A therapeutic massage is also a great tool to release stress and help you process through your healing.

At this point, I need to explain a bit about Reiki. I am a Reiki Master/Teacher, having taught all three levels of Reiki for many years. I am also an active advocate for Reiki. I believe in it so much that I include it in all of my healing sessions. Through Reiki treatments with my clients, I have witnessed many healing benefits.

Reiki is a Japanese method used for centuries to promote physical healing, stress reduction, relaxation, and healing on many levels.

This method is performed by holding the hands over or directing energy toward someone and using symbols to channel this universal energy. The healer is taught and attuned to this method of healing by a Reiki Master.

The symbols channel a powerful healing energy from a Higher Power to bring emotional, physical and mental healing of the body. Reiki can be used on people as well as animals and plants. The energy of Reiki cannot hurt you in any way; it only benefits you. As an energy from the universe, Reiki is of the highest vibration. Reiki uses the *chakra system* to balance the energy and begin the healing process.

Chakras

Chakras are the power points in your body that God gave you to heal yourself.

They are like generators that hold and recharge the life force energy that God gives us to exist. Through quantum physics, modern science is beginning to understand the ancient teachings, that energy flows down from the higher-self into the body's seven energy centers known as *chakras*. Physicians have not only acknowledged the existence of *chakras*, but are now able to identify them in the human body.

The word *chakra* means "wheel" in Sanskrit. When I work with the body, I see these wheels being like small motors, recharging the energy of the body. Stress, illness, negativity, or trauma can cause your *chakras* to become blocked. At this point, your body begins to function at a lower vibrational level.

If the life force energy is not flowing correctly, your body cannot function at full capacity. You may see the signs of this diminished energy flow; such as memory loss, fatigue, the inability to release stress, low immune system, disease, depression or anxiety. All of these are signs that the body is giving to you, telling you that something is wrong. The body's energy system is blocked.

There are seven major *chakras* in the body, and one or more of your *chakras* can be partially to completely blocked or shutdown, creating this stress on your body.

Here is an example of your *chakra* system. It may be an unusual way of seeing it, but I worked in the electrical contracting field for many years and this comparison helped me.

Imagine the electrical wiring in your house. You have many plug outlets and light outlets that draw energy. There is a circuit box with individual circuit breakers that control the energy going to each group of outlets. When you overload one group of outlets, it will trip the circuit breaker, causing the electricity to stop flowing to those outlets. Instead of correcting the problem (dealing with the issue) and resetting the breaker, we may just get out the extension cord and plug all of those items into another circuit, eventually overloading it as well.

Some of us do this to the point that all of our circuits are shut down, and instead of calling an electrician to discover and fix the problem, we try to run an extension cord to our neighbor's house. Think of your body as the circuit box, your *chakras* the circuit breakers, and the electrical outlets are your body's emotional, mental and physical systems. To meet the needs of our existence, we plug into our outlets.

If we do not correct the electrical overload by dealing with the stress, trauma or grief, our whole electrical energy flow eventually shuts down.

When we create excessive stress on the emotional, mental or physical level of the body, our *chakra* motors begin struggling, and less energy is generated by them. Each *chakra* provides energy to different parts of the body. When a *chakra* becomes completely blocked, a weakness is created in that area, making it vulnerable to illness or injury.

Some of our blockages are created early in childhood, being related to the emotional memories and trauma the child carries.

The emotional damage of relationships as well as physical injuries, illness or surgeries can block *chakras*. Grief is a particularly powerful emotion that connects to many other emotions, all of which can affect the blockage of *chakras*. Mental stress can also overload a *chakra,* causing it to become unbalanced or to begin shutting down.

We all have blockages that occur in our *chakras* at one time or another. That is why it is important to listen to your body and to be aware of how it is functioning.

I am sure you are wondering, "What do I do about my blocked chakras?" That is what Reiki and other energy work does. It helps your body to begin clearing and releasing the negative energy that is causing the blockage. Your body was designed by God to heal itself. If your *chakras*, these energy generators in your body, are working at full capacity, then this self-healing is possible. Yoga, Tai Chi, meditation, and exercise are all excellent tools to maintain the balance of your *chakras*. Some type of energy work may be necessary to do the initial clearing and releasing of blocked energy before you can maintain them properly.

This information is provided to educate you on what is actually going on with your body, mind, and spirit.

The seven *chakras* are located down the center line of the human body. Here is a basic description of them.

1st – Root *Chakra* – Red – Located at the base of the spine between the legs;

2nd – Sacral and Sexual *Chakra* – Orange – Located near or below the waist;

3rd – Solar Plexus *Chakra* – Yellow – located just above waist;

4th – Heart *Chakra* – Green – Located in the center of the chest;

5th – Throat *Chakra* – Blue – Located in the throat area;

6th – Third Eye *Chakra* – Indigo or Deep blue – located in center of forehead;

7th – Crown *Chakra* – Purple – Located on top of the head.

This is just a small sample of information about Reiki and *Chakras.* I strongly encourage you to read more about both subjects. The healing method of Reiki can be taught to anyone. To do Reiki for yourself and others, you must be taught the symbols and be attuned by a Reiki Master/Teacher. To experience Reiki, however, and open the blockages in your *chakras,* you need only to relax and undergo the healing touch of a Reiki practitioner.

Here are a couple of my clients' comments about the healing power of Reiki.

I've had psychic abilities all of my life. For me they just came naturally, and I didn't realize there was anything astonishing about them for a long time. I "channeled" my time and concentration into music, which was also a talent and ambition for me.

Musical and writing talentss ran strongly in my father's side of the family, and it was certainly more acceptable to be a musician or teacher than a teenage psychic! I realized at some point that I often knew things that were going to happen, or I could pick up information by just holding a picture or object and "zoning"– letting the object talk to me. However, I often thought this was just my imagination–especially when others scoffed as I warned them about something. Later, it would indeed happen, but they were usually just angry and unsettled by my accuracy.

So, in a sense, I learned to repress and ignore my messages concerning others, deliberately trying to "tune it out." This didn't stop my psychic gift from operating— I just kept it to myself.

Then, one day, some friends asked me to go with them to a psychic fair in town. I thought it would be fun and I needed something to either distract me or cheer me up.

I was a passionate gay Christian who couldn't seem to fit into any church. I was completely rejected by the last pastor I had tried to work with, and I had recently undergone a painful separation and breakup with someone I loved dearly and had trusted.

I was confused and hurting. In addition, several of my longtime friends had become estranged as a result of the breakup and my partner's influence over them. I felt abandoned by people and by God. As a member of the "walking wounded," I rambled around the fair, with not much hope or expectation that anyone there could help me. But, it felt safe to be there. The spiritual energy felt positive—nothing dark or hocus pocus! I was drawn to Linda's table where she was doing "chakra cleansing." I kind of laughed to myself. "Chakra cleansing! Good grief. She just looks like someone's Mom to me…" Yet, she had a quiet and focused manner. Very intriguing. Besides, I ought not to laugh. I knew my chakras had to be pretty messed up! I decided to go over and sign up.

Within a few minutes, I was on a massage table and she was standing over me, scanning her hands over my entire body, stopping now and then. She had a breathing technique that sounded like the wind, as I felt the energy from her hands. She would pull out "gunk" and toss it aside while infusing me with positive, healing energy. It wasn't just ANY kind of energy. I knew it was from the Divine. I later learned this method of healing was Reiki. She then began to tell me things and ask me things. "Who are these seven people I see standing in a line with their back turned to you?" It was the seven people who I felt had scorned and abandoned me, including my former partner.

"They cannot rise to where you are, but you should not try to go to where they are either." She also saw my deceased father and described him well. He was encouraging me and wanting me to keep going and get to writing. He was happy and protective and proud. Linda said my only real block at the time was in my heart. I was experiencing a terrible pain there.

When I left the session, I could feel energy shifting in me, both physically, emotionally and on a psychic plane. That day marked a dramatic turning point in my healing. I began to "collect" myself and rise above my pain. I began to discover and embrace my own God-given gifts again. It dawned on me that my mother had tremendous psychic and healing abilities and I probably inherited much of what I had from her.

Then, a series of things happened the next year challenging me to use my spiritual/psychic abilities. Not the least of which was having active but friendly ghosts in my new home! I continue to have sessions with Linda and have referred many of my friends to her because I know she has a remarkable Reiki gift as well as her channeling abilities.

*Childhood traumas were healed and peace attained with my loved ones who had passed on. I think Linda is especially blessed by God, because of her compassion, honesty and lack of self-serving ego. She is generous in her kindness and desire to truly help others. God led me to her and her to me so we could learn from each other. She is a colleague, a friend and a mentor. She truly opened up my psychic channels, and for this I am so grateful. I now more fully understand who I am and **how** the pieces of my life fit together.*

Five years after my first session with Linda Drake, my own life and work continues to expand miraculously. As they say, "the sky is the limit!" With God, perhaps there is no limit.

L.B. Austin

Here is another testimonial from a gentleman who experienced the power of Reiki at a health fair.

Linda, the first time I went to your booth and got within 15 feet of you I began to experience peace and calmness, something that I had not felt in a long time. There are no words to describe the feeling, but after you explained to me what Reiki was, I knew I had to try it.

At this time of my life I was experiencing intense pain in my shoulders, clavicles, hands and knees. The doctors told me they were signs of arthritis. After the Reiki session, I felt like a hundred bucks. Later in the week, I noticed that my pain and aches were still gone. I knew I had run into the presence of someone special. After taking Reiki classes and sessions from you, not only has my health improved, but also I have noticed something in me has shifted to a more positive outlook about how I view the world and myself.

J. L. El Paso

This first session of Reiki was only the beginning. It cleared his *chakras* to begin the releasing process, enabling him to start healing the anger that he carried.

When working with this gentleman, we discovered that the pain in his body actually represented the anger he held against his father. He felt stuck and controlled as he struggled against what he viewed as a helpless situation. We released the anger that was keeping his life blocked. That releasing and healing of belief systems empowered him to take control of his life.

I am pleased to say he is a very different man today. His life has totally changed and he just glows with confidence that he did not have before.

Healing Yourself

Giving you the tools and the methods to heal yourself is the purpose of this book. In the previous chapters, I have described these tools and methods that can be useful in attaining health, meaningful relationships, and achieving your life's purpose.

We have now put them into a plan, so that you can successfully implement them into your life.

There are several steps that you must go through to achieve the full effect you need to use them all. I did not say this healing work would be easy or that it could be achieved over night! It will take work and determination. But the benefits will bring you closer to the dreams and desires of your life.

Also, let me emphasize, although I am talking about a self-help method of identifying and healing your issues, you may need the help of others – those in your soul group, a healer/facilitator or even professionals, including professional counselors. Begin each step with a prayer for clarity and healing.

STEP ONE: Begin your healing process by clearing your entire body with Reiki or another method of clearing. The more open you are the easier it is to release blocked energy and negative belief systems. You may also want to try a meditation that focuses on opening your chakra system. Reiki may not be available to you at this time, so don't delay, just ask your angels to open and clear your energy so that you can receive the healing, as this is also effective.

STEP TWO: Start a journal. It doesn't have to be fancy or expensive. It doesn't even have to have correct spelling and punctuation! A notebook will do, or you can even do it on a computer if you are so inclined. Remember that your journal is a gift that you are giving yourself—the empowering gift of healing your life, allowing you to have the happiness and success that you desire.

You must stay focused on that thought, or you will begin to allow other things to get in the way of your journaling time, denying your healing and causing you to get stuck right back where you were.

Journaling is a very important tool since it allows you to communicate in ways that you may never have done before. You will also find it to be a record of not only your deepest thoughts and emotions, but also confirmation of your healing progress as you go back and read your previous entries. Remember to date your entries.

As you progress with your journaling tool, you will discover who you really are and what your needs are.

I have found that we often deny ourselves expression of our emotional needs. We may do this for so long that we forget what these needs are or feel that we are not worthy of having emotional needs. This suppression causes us to become discontent, angry, moody, and depressed. Consequently, we also make all of those around us miserable. We soon become so disconnected from who we really are that we cannot find our true path.

The further disconnected we become from our higher-selves and our path, the more we create discontent and struggle in our paths.

It is necessary that you release all fears of someone else reading your journal, since it is just for you. If you are concerned about the privacy of your journal, please keep it locked away in a safe place. As you begin, you will see yourself opening up and becoming better and better at it, until soon your journal becomes your best friend and confidant. I encourage you to write in it every day or at a minimum of every other day. You may start with a page, but soon you will find yourself writing multiple pages.

1. How do you write a journal?

Allow time. Begin by allowing yourself a minimum of 30 minutes each day. Don't cut yourself short—this time is for you! If you write for 10 minutes and then can't think of anything else to say, use the remainder of the time for prayer or meditation.

I cannot overemphasize the necessity for prayer and meditation as you write! Ask your angels and spirit guides to assist you.

2. What do you say?

If you don't have much to say, write about a memory from your childhood, since you are practicing getting in touch with your emotions.

At this point, you may be wondering what you could possibly write about each day. I did the same thing. You will be surprised at the things you will begin to share with your private journal. You may start by telling about the things you did that day, conversations you had, thoughts and emotions that came to mind as you went through the events of your day. You will soon find yourself using your journal to vent thoughts and emotions that you would not dare express to others.

3. How does a journal work as a healing tool?

It tells you who you are. As time passes, go back and read what you have been writing. You will begin to see that you are expressing your emotional needs, your memories, all those things you may have never told a living soul. You have to find out who you are to begin healing yourself!

Another way of using journaling as a healing tool is this: as you are going through your healing process, you will turn back to previous situations with the same experiences to reflect on how you may have changed your reactions and emotions. This is part of breaking our old patterns. It is at that time that you will stand up and cheer at the changes you have made in your life.

STEP THREE: Discover your life purpose.

Discovering your life purpose needs to be done in a separate notebook. The time spent on this project cannot be counted as part of your journaling time because it will take much longer.

We first begin with your childhood. Throughout this book you have seen how frequently I have referred to your childhood as the beginning of your experiences with your issues. Now it is time to start identifying your issues to discover your life purpose. These are **your** issues. You chose them, but we will assist you in gaining a better understanding of them.

Some of the issues you chose may include Trust, Abandonment, Abuse, Control, Judgment, Love and Responsibility. All of these issues affect the image we hold of ourselves.

I have shared many examples of issues throughout this book to enable you to better identify your own issues.

- Our issues create experiences that form our emotional memories.
- Through these emotional memories a belief system is developed.
- That belief system creates blockages that form patterns (the repeating of an action), and these patterns are demonstrated through experiences of our life.
- These patterns enable us to continue experiencing our issues until we heal the negative emotion that the issue creates within us. Thus, we have achieved our life purpose in healing that issue.

Let us begin our work on the **Life Purpose Notebook**:

1. Look back at your childhood. How was one or more of these issues demonstrated through the experiences of your childhood? Write down the issue and then think: How was it demonstrated and by whom? Do one issue at a time, working all the way through it, coming back at another time to do the next one. We will come back to process the emotions connected to them later in this process.

2. What is your belief system about yourself? What beliefs did you establish because of the emotional memories connected to this issue? List those beliefs.

3. Then, ask yourself, how have those beliefs created blockages in your life? Example: If I'm not perfect who could love me? Do you sabotage relationships or deny yourself a relationship believing you are not good enough or do not deserve it? List the blockages.

4. What patterns have you created because of this belief? List the patterns.

5. How have those patterns affected your life, blocking happiness, love, or success?

6. How have these patterns repeated in your life? In relationships–Family? Friends? Intimate relationships? Career? Financially?

When you have finished with the first relationship, begin with the next one until you have worked through all of your significant relationships and the issues, beliefs and patterns associated with those relationships. You may even enlist a close friend to assist you as their perception can sometimes give you clarity in uncovering hidden issues.

You can use this guide in your journal:

- Name of Person:
- Issue or issues they challenged you with:
- What words or emotions were experienced in the relationship:
- Childhood memories–both positive and negative: Pay attention to what emotions come up with the memories and note these emotions.
- Ask your inner-child what significant memories he/she would like to heal. The adult memories may be different

than the child's and the more you work with the child the more he or she will reveal to you, as a trust is built.

- What beliefs did you establish because of the emotional memories connected to this issue? (See beliefs attached to each issue chapter.)

- What blockages have these beliefs created for you in my relationships or career? Note them one by one, *i.e.: I am working below my potential for fear of failure. I broke up my relationship with Jim because of fear of commitment. I don't have friendships for fear of abandonment. (Use personal experiences)*

- What patterns have you created in your life because of this issue or belief? You can sabotage your life with negative patterns, *i.e.: I attract abusive relationships. I fear abandonment so I stay in relationships when I know they aren't working for me. I can't keep a job, I don't trust people, I resist or resent authority.*

- What negative emotion around this issue do you need to change or overcome to have the life that you desire?

- How can you forgive this person?

It is truly not necessary to do forgiveness work in-person. Most of the time it is just not possible. You are the one that needs to heal, as the pain or fear experienced in your childhood is still affecting **your** life in a detrimental way. The person that you experienced your issue with usually has no awareness of the negative emotions created by their actions. They are typically the same person they've always been, treating you, as the adult, in the same they did when you were the child. They typically have no desire to change, as they do not see their actions as a problem so pursuing the change in them is futile.

The change must occur in you. This is your responsibility in healing yourself to create an improved, happier and more fulfilled life. All of this involves self-love as that propels you to do this healing work.

This entire relationship was created by your higher-self to help you grow and evolve on a human and spiritual level. Having forgiveness and gratitude for the devotion of these two spirits to works together to achieve this spiritual evolution is truly love.

Of course, in your journal you will need plenty of writing space for each question as you may come back to each person multiple times but this provides you with an example of the worksheet you can use to process through your relationships, issues and negative emotional memories.

Linda's note If using a notebook, I suggest a five subject spiral one so that each relationship has it's own section. Most of you have plenty to write.

STEP FOUR: Learn, and use, **forgiveness**.

The next tool I will give you is forgiveness. You must work with forgiveness.

1. Forgiving yourself for choosing such difficult issues.
2. Forgiving others (family, spouses and friends) for creating the experiences for you.
3. Forgiving God for allowing those things to happen to you (Remember, God had nothing to do with your choices).

Now that you have identified your issues, your beliefs, and your patterns, you have the ability to change the experiences of your life.

You cannot change your issue, since that is part of your life purpose.

Through working with this method, however, you can heal your emotional memories, changing your belief system so that you can take control of how you feel about yourself. This will also give you control of your patterns. Because your belief system will have changed, the pattern of the experiences that you attract will also change.

You will continue to experience situations with your issues, but because of your knowledge and healing work, you have gained control over the outcome of the situation.

The results of this healing work can be phenomenal!

STEP FIVE: When do you need professional counseling?

As I've explained, it is necessary for you to heal with the person with whom your emotional memories were created. This may be a challenging task, and if you cannot successfully work through it by yourself, seek out help through alternative methods or professional counseling.

Staying stuck in this pain is not mentally or physically healthy for you and those around you. Take action in valuing yourself enough to get help. (Pardon the slang word (stuck) but Abraham said it was a word everyone would understand.)

There may be many of you who still have the injured child within you. This inner-child does not understand any of the theory of this healing, but it holds the trauma of its childhood deep within its soul and it wants to heal. If this is your situation, I strongly recommend a trained facilitator or therapist. You will need assistance in dealing with the flood of emotion that must be released from the child. There are many different methods available for doing this work. I recommend you do some research and get referrals before making your choice.

When a client comes to me, I never know what to expect. It is their life and their journey, and we all have choices to make along our paths. We provide each client with the knowledge and tools to change their life and it is their responsibility to do the work in the time frame that they desire.

Here is a story from a client who took her responsibility seriously and how her work changed her life.

I began working with Linda in January of 2005. When I went to my first appointment, I thought I was there to have my tarot cards read and to have some insight into my future. Little did I know that this was only the beginning of an amazing life-changing journey. On this first appointment I learned that we all come into this life with a preconceived plan. We choose the issues that we would like to address and then through our personal choices we experience them at different levels, with the ultimate goal being to learn from them.

I learned that I came into this life to experience seven out of the seven major issues. The issues were judgment, abandonment, love, abuse, control, trust and responsibility. I could no longer avoid looking at my "stuff." My issues were now in my face. I began seeing Linda regularly to address them. My partner began her work with Linda a month later. We both certainly had our work cut out for us.

When I came to Linda I was angry, confused and anxiety-ridden. I had been playing out my issues in all of my close relationships. My love relationship was being severely affected and on the brink of being over. My son was in a boarding school for troubled teens. My daughter had become withdrawn. As far as my parents were concerned, I felt angry and resentful believing that it was their fault I had always been such a mess.

Linda, Spirit and I began working with my angry (inner child) little girl. I began to work through the anger towards my parents and come to a place of forgiveness.

I now know that I chose my parents before I was conceived. I chose them to help me experience my issues and to learn from them. As a child,

I remember the unhappiness that we all felt. My parents were either indifferent to each other or they were fighting. They decided they needed "something" to help put the family back together. They decided to adopt a child. When I was five years old my parents adopted my four-year-old brother. I could not understand, why? There wasn't enough love for me; now I had to share. I remember thinking that just maybe this would make my parents happy. It didn't help. By the end of my third grade year my parents decided to get a divorce. I just felt numb.

My mother, brother and I moved to a new house after the divorce. My mother was emotionally unavailable. I would sit outside her bedroom door just waiting for her to notice me. So here I was in the fourth grade with a brother that was basically a stranger and two parents who had abandoned me. A year later my mother remarried. My stepfather decided early in our relationship that I was the enemy so he became very abusive. I was confined to my room most of the time so that he didn't have to look at me. He made sure that we all knew that he was in control. After a couple of years my mother and step-father got a divorce and we moved back to our previous house.

As a teenager, I was very self-destructive. I was just so angry that I had a huge chip on my shoulder. I didn't trust anyone. I was searching for something that was "real". I wanted so desperately to love and be loved. I turned to drugs, alcohol and promiscuity.

My best friend and I were on the roller coaster ride of life pledging to be each other's family. We both felt so alone and yet together. We never planned on the next set of events. The summer before our senior year in high school, my best friend was killed in a car accident. I felt as if I was being punished and I would frequently ask my mother "Why is God doing this to me?" I was getting to experience abandonment once again.

I thought okay, I give in. If I go to church and become a "good" Christian maybe then I could find peace. I became very involved in the church. I sang in the choir and I was basically there anytime the doors were open, all the while, still engaging in self-destructive behaviors in private.

At the age of 18 I married one of my suitors. It was a marriage of convenience. We both wanted independence from our families so we decided to play grown ups. We had two children by the time I was 22. At the age of 24 my marriage had run its course, so the kids and I moved in with my mother. I had become a shell of a person. I felt that God had forsaken me once again. This is where the responsibility issue comes in. I could not stand the person that I had become. I started hanging out in bars again drinking and drugging, hoping to numb the pain. I had become totally disconnected. My mother had taken over my parenting responsibilities. I was living in the house with my mother and children however "nobody was home" in my mind or my heart. This behavior continued for at least a year.

The turning point for me was upon realizing that I had been living in denial for years. I was afraid to be judged. I had the realization that I was and am a lesbian. I had clearly been denying this possibility for a long time. This new found awareness was the step needed to help with my identity crisis. In life each of us experiences judgment in different ways and at different times. I certainly have judged others, whether it was how someone dressed or looked, how they chose to practice their religious beliefs or even their political views. If their choices were different from mine, I tended to place some judgment on them.

This lesson was definitely life changing. I was now experiencing other people's judgment ten-fold. I lost most of my so-called friends and my family relationships became very strained.

By my early thirties I had cleaned up my life the best I knew how. I had been seeing a therapist for years and I had identified how everyone's role in our family had affected me. I still had so much anger, fear, and resentment that I didn't know what to do with.

During this time, I went through the ending of what I thought was the most meaningful relationship of my life. Once again I cried to my mother "Why has God forsaken me, he said he wouldn't give us more than we can bear." I will never forget the look of love and wisdom that I saw in my mother's eyes. She had found some peace. She said to me, "You have forgotten the most important part of that scripture. He said he would never give us more than we can bear without him." I realized at that moment it wasn't God that had abandoned me; it was I that had abandoned Him.

I continued to experience hardships of varying degrees. The difference being, now I had faith. At the age of 35 I met the love of my life and over the next couple of years we set out to make a life together. We were struggling to live together as a family. During this time, my son had gotten himself into the same self-destructive game that I had played. My partner and I discussed our options and I then made the most difficult, loving decision of my life. We admitted my son into a facility for troubled teens. Thank God for my faith during these trying times. I cried a lot! My daughter stayed in her room most of the time as this had become her safe haven. My partner and I were now discussing separating.

This is where Linda and Spirit come in. Working with Spirit I learned that I chose this life and all seven issues to experience with the family that I had chosen. I have found forgiveness for my parents but most importantly for myself. This realization helped me to release the anger and resentment that I had carried around for years. I now have a loving communicative relationship with both of my parents. I have been able to put the difficult relationship my brother and I have had into perspective. I can now say that I learned a lot from him. We were both just trying to survive.

My partner and I have learned how we were "playing" out our issues in our relationship. We each now have the awareness and the "tools" to address situations as they arise. The love that we share is more than I could have ever imagined. For the first time in my life, I feel safe and loved.

Both of my kids have worked with Linda as well. My son completed his program and is now in college. My daughter has blossomed, doing well in school with plans for college. I can honestly say that I have become the mother they can and do respect. I had to really work to forgive myself for not being the mother I thought I should have been. The forgiveness came when I realized they chose me! I now try to be supportive and loving yet, this is a hard one; I have learned that I have to release the control and let them learn their life lessons along the way. That is why we are here!

I am a continuing work in progress with a new life direction. I am pursuing an education to be an ordained Spiritualist minister with the vision of giving back what I have been given; an ever developing sense of peace.

Since Chris began addressing and healing the challenges in her life, she has opened up to fulfill her spiritual purpose. She has embraced her spiritual gifts to bless the lives of others with her amazing healing abilities and mediumship abilities. I look forward to witnessing all that Chris will become without the limitations of her negative beliefs.

CHAPTER 12
RELATIONSHIPS: WHY THEY ARE SO IMPORTANT

A relationship–what is it really?

A relationship is two people drawn together in family, friendship, business or an intimate bond, providing us the opportunity to experience our issues. These opportunities are the purpose of our life plan. Our issues are what each lifetime is about. Through our relationships, we can discover our issues, the beliefs formed by them, and the patterns we repeat. These patterns will create challenges for us, and through these challenges, we have the opportunity to learn, change, and grow. Get excited about this opportunity as this is your life purpose.

Our relationships create the stage, complete with characters and props, to experience our issues. The child carries the script created by it's higher-self with all of it's issues into this life, understanding this is the part he is supposed to play–but not understanding that he has the power to change the patterns of his reactions, thus changing the outcome.

As humans, the relationship connection is vital to our existence. Our first experience starts with the relationship between parent and child.

It expands to include our family circle, then into the outside world of friendships. We eventually come to the point where we are ready for a more intimate relationship.

We are all looking for the one "perfect" relationship. We dream of the perfect relationship, with no disagreements, obstacles, or challenges. There is no such thing! It is not reality—it is a dream, a fantasy, that many search their entire lives to find.

Many relationships crumble simply because they are an illusion that cannot stand up to the pressures of the real world. A great relationship is about two individuals coming together, each in their own power, accepting the other's differences, yet still loving the other. This is not an easy task!

It is through your relationships that you are allowed to experience your issues of trust, abuse, abandonment, control, judgment, responsibility, and love. These issues are capable of creating major negative relationship experiences. But, if that was not enough, you carry all of your emotional memories from childhood into your present relationships. It is no wonder that a great relationship is so much work! Every relationship that you have is perfect, as it is divinely formulated for the opportunity to gain knowledge, heal karma and advance the soul. It is your negative beliefs that separate you from the unconditional love of God.

It is through the energy of your desires and intent that you are able to co-create with God. Your daily thoughts, whether negative or positive, propel your life in that direction.

You will probably have many relationships—partners, family, and friends. With everyone having many issues to resolve, it is often difficult for relationships to hold up to the pressure of working through all of these issues. This is especially true when you do not understand the purpose of the relationships.

Too often, we have the same relationship over and over again—just with different people.

You repeatedly experience your unresolved issues with your emotional memories, beliefs, and patterns in multiple relationships, yet you expect different outcomes. Without working with the knowledge of your issues, your patterns will not change, your karma will not be healed and your life will continue the same painful path. Remember, it was through agreement that you came into this life with this person. They are only fulfilling their obligation to your life plan and you to theirs. For most, the healing plan we have given you up to this point will enable you to move forward with your life, making the necessary changes.

Forgiveness is an essential part to all the healing that you need. Focus on the perfection of all that is and begin creating it.

To be a part of a truly great relationship, you must be able to experience the challenges of both party's issues. We all came into this life to work on our issues. These experiences are what relationships are about. A great relationship is having someone who cares enough to endure the trauma of working with you through the experiences of your issues. That is the person who is right for you, at least at that time. The other side of the coin is that you have to care enough about that person to be there for him while he works through his issues. Then you are the right person for him. (Remember, these pronouns are not gender-specific!)

The combination of both parties' work can involve multiple lessons, as well a large amount of patience to endure this work. Sound like fun? And you've spent years looking for this relationship, right?

Remember, it is through prearrangement with those of your soul group to interact with you at a specific time and space in your life to most efficiently experience these issues. There are no coincidences.

You agreed with many souls to help one another with your issues, and to heal karmic energy created in past lives. As you travel your life's path, you are drawn to these souls. Their issues coordinate with yours. Our proverbial puzzle of life involves each of us connecting with others, each fitting into the right spot, at the right time, to complete the perfect picture of the puzzle of life.

As I've stated many times throughout this book, your issues are first activated when you are a child.

Looking back, as children, some of you may have had the controlling father or mother whom you could not please. No matter what you did or how you did it, they decided whether it was good enough, and it seemed to that child like it never was. The child soon lost faith in himself, and decided at a young age that love was about control and judgment.

The belief was created that he needed someone to take care of him, and thus control him. The child then grew to believe that he was not powerful enough to control his (or her) own life.

As the child matures into the adult, he searches for someone to take care of him in the same way the controlling parent did. This adult will unknowingly search for someone with control issues much like the parent. After all, control is what he identifies with love. As an adult, he or she will be drawn to a relationship with a controlling partner—until they find their power and break loose of the shackles.

Unfortunately, this control issue is very difficult to overcome without help. The adult may release himself from this relationship, but then all too often find him self in a similar one. This is their issue, and they will be given numerous opportunities to experience it through many relationships. There is hope!

They can heal their need to continue experiencing the patterns of this issue. Through knowledge, they can learn to release and make conscious changes to their choices. Through acknowledgment and empowerment, they can change the need to repeat the experience. You are empowered to make changes to your life through love. If the love does not come from others, it must come from self. This is your responsibility: to accomplish your soul's purpose.

Many people come to me asking if it is wrong to divorce an abusive partner or if they are destined to remain in the painful situation. Their cultural or religious beliefs confuse them as to what they need to do. This is a decision that each individual must make for himself. God does not punish you by condemning you to a situation such at this.

Your spirit chose the experience as an opportunity for you to learn about and overcome the negative belief that created the situation. Just because you chose the lesson does not justify staying in the situation.

The lesson is learned through loving and valuing yourself, releasing any negative beliefs that prevent you from setting boundaries, and working to overcome the situation allowing you to take back your power. This is where you have an opportunity to find your strength and to overcome the negativity of the relationship. The relationship will not change without your efforts.

If you are allowing yourself to be in an abusive relationship, is this demonstrating love of self? Whether the abuse is physical, emotional or verbal, it is still harmful to your self-worth.

A judgmental or controlling partner may not realize or care about the damage they are doing to others with their actions.

Without realizing it, you gave away your power by allowing this person to treat you in this way. You may have done this out of love for this person or maybe this was done in an attempt to earn their love. It is your responsibility to learn the lesson of setting boundaries and teaching others how to demonstrate love to you.

It is your belief system that you are actually challenged with. A belief system was established earlier in your life that convinced you that it is acceptable for others to treat you in an abusive, disrespectful way.

Typically it is an overwhelming fear that causes you to remain in a dysfunctional relationship. Maybe it is fear of abandonment, judgment, control or the biggest fear of all, the fear of the unknown. You must evaluate the situation and determine what you want for your life. There is help available for you through local agencies when you are ready to take back your power. You must know and believe that you deserve positive, loving, supportive relationships. It is important to love yourself before anyone else to have a healthy relationship.

When you begin to take back your power, you want to enlist the most supportive of your family and friends and encircle yourself with their love.

In the beginning, I told you this book would be all about you. I hope we have given you a better understanding of yourself, your issues and your relationships. To present this book in the way Abraham desired, they presented their knowledge through me, our experiences, and the true-life experiences of our clients, we hope this enabled you to easily apply the knowledge to your life.

With this knowledge, you have the ability to create all that you desire within your life. Life is not about suffering. It is about overcoming challenges to find your joy. Envision what you desire, set your intent with the universe and take the responsibility for creating it.

Healing relationships and teaching others to love you will be the subject of the next book in our healing series. See you then!

Spirit, Abraham & Linda

Made in the USA
San Bernardino, CA
05 April 2014